Gonell —
Dance = magic!

# The Irish Witch's Dress

# The Irish Witch's Dress

## Rod Vick

Laikituk Creek Publishing

# The Irish Witch's Dress

Laikituk Creek Publishing

Manufactured in the United States of America.

ISBN: 978-0-6922-8840-5

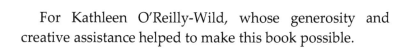

For Kathleen O'Reilly-Wild, whose generosity and creative assistance helped to make this book possible.

# What readers are saying about Rod Vick's Irish dance-themed fiction...

'Hello Mr. Vick - I'm happy to say my daughter has finally become addicted to books.'
- *Kristin Tousignant, Windsor, Ontario*

'Here is a book every aspiring dancer should read.'
- *Hornpipe Magazine on Kaylee's Choice*

'Rod Vick's stories are always honest and heartwarming...writing that gets better every book!'
- *Kathleen O'Reilly-Wild, Feis America Magazine*

'Motivational...inspiring...Finally, dancers can identify with their own hero.'
- *Irish Dance Magazine*

'Vick does an amazing job of creating suspense. I found myself rushing through other tasks to get back to my reading.'
- *Christy Dorrity, review of*
*Dancer in the Painted Mask in Irish Central*

'We've both got the whole set. I order them online for the next big gift occasion as soon as they're out!'
- *Jill Hynes, Ontario, Canada*

'I think the concept and the book are brilliant.'
- *Jeff Winke, author of The PR Idea Book on Kaylee's Choice*

'Please keep writing!'
- *Brianna Thompson, Michigan parent*

.

## Author's Note

*This story contains many references to Celtic mythology, although I have modified some details relating to the strange beings and their powers. If other authors are permitted to make vampires sparkle, I suppose I can take a few liberties.*

# Part I

*Ireland*
*Late Summer 1947*

## *Katie's Tale*
# The Night Visitors

## 1

"We must keep our voices very low, lest they hear us," said John O'Malley to his eleven-year-old daughter. The two of them sat on the edge of her bed in the dark loft of the farm house. Had someone approached them from behind, the pair would have appeared to be staring at nothing at all, for their faces hovered inches from the painted wall boards. However, their eyes were actually fixed on a thin opening where a plank had shrunk, creating a viewing sliver that overlooked the kitchen and dining areas below.

"I don't see anything," whispered Katie.

"There's nothing to see—yet," said her father. "If they come, you'll know it. They usually arrive around midnight."

Katie knew the time must be close. She had gone to bed two hours ago, as had her mother, who slept in the large bedroom downstairs. Her father had come up and awakened her—as he had promised—just a few minutes ago. Katie still felt heavy with sleep, but excited, too. She had never seen *them* before, had always thought them the creation of adult storytellers bent on frightening or disciplining children.

A part of her wondered whether this was her father's mission as well. He had already told her they did not come every night, which provided a ready excuse if midnight arrived without the creatures. Yet, it was not like her father to spin yarns as a means of encouraging her cooperation.

But still...could something so fantastic be true? A shiver shook her. Although she wore a cotton nightgown that hung from her auburn curls to her toes, she now pulled the quilt from the bed around her shoulders as well.

"You're shaking," observed her father, speaking just loudly enough for her ears to hear. "Are you frightened?"

"Just cold," she whispered, although this was only partially true.

"You don't have anything to worry about, you know," he said. "The stone is ready. There won't be any mischief."

Although she could not see it in the dark, Katie had watched her father drizzle honey into a hole in the center of a flat stone that now sat on a bench in front of the hearth. A gift for the visitors. He had also left a bowl of milk.

Yet, as the minutes ticked by and she became more fully awake, Katie began to have second thoughts about their adventure. It frightened her to think that there might be a world of extraordinary beings that, under certain conditions, intersected with her own world. It occurred to Katie that if she crawled back into bed right now and succeeded in falling asleep, she could continue to pretend the creatures did not exist. Once she saw them, however, she would always have the knowledge that, on some nights, they were right there in her house while she and her parents slept.

Another shudder.

Katie was about to say *Maybe they're not coming* and had begun to inch her way back onto the center of the mattress, when she detected a slight movement in the darkness of the kitchen, something so subtle that she would have easily missed it had her eyes not been straining into the moonlight-tinged darkness for the past quarter-hour. Then she detected another movement and a soft sliding sound as a window opened. A dozen small bodies scrambled almost noiselessly across the sill, one bearing a glass lamp within which burned a candle. This bathed the room in a subtle, golden glow and offered a better look at the visitors. Katie bit down on a corner of the quilt to prevent herself from accidentally crying out.

The visitors had two arms and two legs, like humans, but were roughly one-third the size of a man, with skin the color of the full moon. Their eyes were large and dark with almost no whites showing, their fingers slender and nimble. They moved with the swiftness and grace of children, though their limbs were sinewy like working men, and their faces appeared ancient and vaguely sad. Katie noticed that all were bald and also bereft of facial hair. Their neat clothing appeared to have been deftly woven from the grasses, ferns and leaves of the surrounding countryside. The mob rushed to the milk bowl and honey stone, lapping from them like starving animals.

Katie moved her lips against her father's ear. "What are they?"

Her father turned his nose into her hair and spoke, almost inaudibly. "Fairies."

Katie's eyes widened. "I thought fairies had wings and were beautiful."

Mr. O'Malley smiled. "Legends say there are many different kinds of fairies. During the day, these fairies live in the streams and meadows. It's only at night that they come into people's houses."

She watched as the fairies finished with the bowl and the stone. Then one of them spoke in a low tone, difficult to hear, yet Katie felt certain it was an unfamiliar tongue. In response, half a dozen began to sweep the floor, pull down cobwebs, scrub the coffee pot, shovel ash from the fireplace. One even sat at Mr. O'Malley's desk, donned a pair of small, wire spectacles, and began paging through Mr. O'Malley's farm records, adding figures here, jotting notes there.   The rest of the fairies scrambled out the window. Katie looked to her father in question.

"They're off to milk the cows, collect the eggs, make repairs. They're workers, all of them. They do it in exchange for the milk and honey."

Katie nodded but then asked, "What if you forget to put out the milk and honey?"

"Oh, then they get upset! They pull pranks. Maybe break a china cup. Hide a favorite book. Put a dead mouse in your shoe so that you find it when you go to slip it on in the morning."

Katie cringed.

"Why do they do it?" she asked. "All the work, I mean."

Her father watched them for a moment before speaking. "I think this race of fairies may owe some sort of debt to men. Probably the result of an ancient war. And I suspect they're not entirely happy about having to pay it. I'll wager that's why they misbehave whenever they are given an excuse."

Katie said nothing. Merely watching the small creatures efficiently clean the house was fascinating.

"But there's something else," her father continued. "I believe the fairies have helped *us* a bit more than they do most people. You see, one night this past spring, howling dogs woke me. Then I heard growling and some commotion out behind the sheds. Grabbed my gun, and when I came around the corner of the byre, there was one of the beasts, baring his teeth at me and struggling with something. Thought he had a chicken, so I shot him. When I came over to take a closer look, I saw it wasn't a chicken at all, but rather one of our little fairies lying on the ground, covered in teeth marks."

Katie let out a sympathetic sigh, and her father had to shush her. She knew packs of wild dogs were rare, but, according to her father, could be dangerous even to humans.

"First time I'd ever seen a fairy, and I had to slap myself in the cheeks a time or two to make sure I wasn't dreaming. I discovered that the little soul was alive, but barely. And unconscious. I carried him back to our house, placed him on a folded up blanket near the fireplace, cleaned his wounds as well as I could. While most of his injuries were bites, there was one rip in his leafy tunic that revealed a very narrow bruise. The leg beneath it appeared to be broken. Not a typical bite injury. I went to the sink to put water in the kettle for some tea for the little fellow, and that was where I noticed a scrap of leafy fabric caught on a nail sticking up from the windowsill. It matched the fabric of the fairy's smock. The unfortunate creature had caught himself on that nail while exiting, and the window had fallen onto his leg, breaking it. That was why he had been caught by the dogs. Usually the fairies are far too quick to be caught. His shattered leg had slowed him down. Naturally I felt awful. If I had fixed that nail earlier, the dog never would have caught him. But that was neither here nor there. I finished bandaging him up, splinted his leg, set some tea and warm broth near him, and tried to get a bit of sleep. When I woke at dawn, he was gone. I fixed the nail, of course. Since then, the fairies seem to have treated us exceptionally well. I suppose they figure I saved the little fellow's life. Or tried to."

He paused here and squinted through the space between the boards, wearing the subtle smile of a man who, despite evidence staring him in the face, still could not believe he had fairies frequently paying visits to his kitchen. Then he leaned back toward his daughter.

"I wanted you to see them because I figured it's time you know. They help keep the farm running, Katie. If anything ever happens to me, you must remember to put out the milk and honey."

"Nothing's going to happen to you," hissed Katie. "So you'll have to keep remembering yourself!"

"Oh, I don't intend to forget," her father continued. "Since your mother got sick, she hasn't been able to help out as much, you know. And her medicines are pretty expensive, so I had to let go the three fellows who had worked here since your grandfather passed, God rest his soul. There's a lot of land and cattle. Without the fairies to help tend to it all, I'd probably have to sell."

This raised another question. "Is the medicine helping?"

Mr. O'Malley smiled kindly. "Do you know what really helps your mother? It's when you dance for her! Oh, how her eyes light up! You're so good and light on your feet and it's almost like she forgets the pain for just a—"

At this point Mr. O'Malley stopped talking, for he realized that, in his enthusiasm, his voice had risen above the level of a whisper. The two squinted through the crack in the wall, but the kitchen was now dark again and as silent as the heart of a stone.

"Will they come back?" asked Katie. "I mean, now that they know we've seen them?"

Mr. O'Malley squeezed her tiny shoulders and tucked her under her blankets.

"I don't know, sweetheart. I don't know."

# 2

Katie peeped through the hole in the wall the following night but saw no sign of the visitors. The night after that was silent as well. Although he said nothing to her, she could see the worry on her father's face.

*Will we have to sell our land and the house? Will we be able to afford mother's medicine? Oh, I wish I hadn't asked father so many questions and made him so excited!*

But after the third night, Katie woke to find something wholly remarkable. In addition to returning to complete their usual chores, Katie and her parents discovered that Mrs. O'Malley's sewing machine, which had sat unused for over a year, had been polished and then threaded with the most radiant gossamer, almost as fine as spiders' silk. And on the chair next to the machine lay a newly-made dress.

"It's like something out of a dream!" exclaimed Mrs. O'Malley, holding it at arm's length. The fabric was dark like the woolen dresses Katie had seen in a few pubs where dancing competitions had been held, except that on the torso of this dress were seven golden gemstones unlike anything they had ever seen.

"I do believe, Katie Erin O'Malley, that this dress is just your size!" said her mother.

Katie stared at the dress, dazzled by the bold gems, but also a bit wary. "Why did they make it? What's it for?"

Then she looked at the seat of the chair and saw what had been hidden beneath the dress.

Dance shoes.

*Did the fairies make those, too? Are the little creatures really that clever?*

"Put them on, Katie!" her mother begged. "I'll bet you'll look like a queen!"

*Did the visitors hear my father when he talked about my dancing?*

She draped the dress over one arm, conducting a more thorough examination. "But…it's so strange!" When she had watched some of the girls dance at a local tavern, their skirts had been dark wool, and their blouses plain white, sometimes covered by a sweater. This dress looked like something a princess might wear.

"Go on, Katie!" said her father. "You'll make your mother happy!"

She excused herself to her parents' room, where she donned the dress and black slippers. When she emerged, her mother gasped and covered her mouth with her cupped hands. "My goodness, I never dreamed to see such a thing!"

Katie blushed, but inside, she felt an odd sensation—not of embarrassment, but of confidence.

"Give us a dance, Katie!" said her father, who began clapping his palm onto his knee in a regular beat. Katie smiled, bowed to them both, and began moving about the kitchen, high on her toes, whirling, leaping, in perfect time to the clapping, a whirl of black and gold that seemed to radiate a light of its own. Finally she stopped, bowed, and ran to her mother's outstretched arms for a hug.

"I've never seen the like of it!" exclaimed her mother. "Why, I think she's every bit as good as that girl who won the county last year!"

Mr. O'Malley shook his head. "I'm not educated enough in the ways of dance to be able to say. But I know I've never seen Katie Erin O'Malley dance any better than that!"

Katie was pretty sure that he was right. When she had danced in the new dress, she had seemed to feel an energy that she had never felt before. *It was surely the thrill of wearing a new dress, nothing more,* she thought, and then wondered rather guiltily whether the excitement of her performance had worn out her mother, who often tired quickly as a result of her illness. However, Mrs. O'Malley seemed uncharacteristically cheerful the rest of the day, working away as she had years ago before her illness, and cooking the family a supper that Katie felt would have been fitting for a holiday.

*She'll probably be in bed all day tomorrow,* thought Katie, but when the next day arrived, her mother was up early, still full of energy.

*Could it be the dress?* Katie wondered. She recalled her father's words that night in the loft: '*Do you know what really helps your mother? It's when you dance for her!*'

Had the fairies created something special? A garment that could actually make her mother well, or at least stronger? Or was it simply coincidence?

When her father came to the breakfast table, and watched his wife glide around the kitchen, his first words were, "Let's have another dance from our Katie in her princess dress! In fact, I think we should have a dance every morning!"

She realized, then, that her father felt the same way she did. *He thinks the dress is helping her!*

Katie was happy to dance for her mother again. She closed herself into her parents' room to change, but as she stood admiring herself in her mother's mirror, she noticed something odd.

*I don't remember those white gemstones being there yesterday.*

When she emerged from the bedroom, her mother said the same thing. Half a dozen new, smaller gems seemed to have appeared on the torso, accenting the seven original golden stones. And the fabric seemed less rough— lighter and not so much like wool anymore.

*Did the visitors do that? Did they make changes to the dress in the middle of the night? Or is the dress changing on its own?*

Or, she wondered, were they simply imagining these differences? Again, Katie danced. She had found it difficult to imagine that she might feel greater perfection than she had the previous day, yet this day's dance seemed to exceed her earlier effort. It was almost as if her mother's joy fed the dress a kind of energy that helped Katie to dance better, and then in turn, the dress fed this healing energy back to her mother.

Mr. O'Malley beamed at his daughter. She also noted that he left a double portion of milk and honey for the visitors that evening.

# 3

As Mrs. O'Malley's health improved, so did the farm's fortunes. By August, Mr. O'Malley had hired a man to help out. His name was Finn, only in his twenties, yet a hard worker as far as Katie could tell, tall with dark hair and prominent cheekbones. Still, there was something about his eyes that made her uneasy. Small dots of ink, they seemed to follow everyone, study every thing.

He watched Katie dance for her mother a few times and seemed mildly intrigued by how much enjoyment Mrs. O'Malley derived from this. However, after awhile, he appeared to lose interest. This was fine with Katie, who did not want him to know about the dress's powers and its extraordinary makers.

For weeks, the farm fell into a comfortable routine. Then, in October, Mrs. O'Malley reported that a silver tray had gone missing. It was not something she used often, and the heirloom had been tucked away in a high cupboard. Mr. O'Malley suggested that she might have misplaced it, and that it would probably turn up eventually. Later that same month, some tools disappeared from the workbench in one of the sheds, and the herd also seemed to be short a cow. Finn had suggested that the missing tools were probably the work of an itinerant who had come by at a time when the door was unlocked. Many people still had not recovered from shortages caused by the war, and so thievery was not unheard of. The cow? Finn went out looking and reported seeing the body of an animal that had fallen into a ravine. Perhaps it was the cow, Finn suggested. However, Mr. O'Malley had not been able to find the area described by his employee.

Then, in November, Mr. O'Malley discovered Finn in the act of taking Grandfather O'Malley's pocket watch from the top drawer of the bedroom bureau where it had been tucked beneath rolled-up stockings. Finn confessed to all of the crimes, and Mr. O'Malley was set to sack him. However, Finn begged forgiveness, tears streaming down his cheeks. He had made bad choices, he admitted. Drinking. Gambling. Men had beaten him, threatening him with worse if he did not pay off his debts. On top of this, he lived with his sister, who had been abandoned by her husband after he had beaten her to the point where she could not hold down a job. She had small children she could not feed, and so Finn had stepped in to try and put some food in their mouths so that they did not have to hunt through trash piles or beg in the streets.

"Show me!" said Mr. O'Malley, and the following day, Finn had taken his employer to a shabby, three-room shack on the edge of town with no electricity or gas. A filthy woman, her face scarred, lay on a bare mattress under a threadbare blanket, sleeping. Two small children who might have gone a month without bathing played listlessly on the skeleton of a broken sofa, its stuffing a distant memory. Mr. O'Malley fought back a tear, pulled some bills from his pocket and thrust them into Finn's hands. "Get them some food and clean them up! And if you ever steal from me again, I'll break your bloody neck!"

A week later, Katie was sent to live with her Aunt Abigail, who had recently endured a childbirth that had nearly killed her. The ordeal had drained Aunt Abigail. Her recovery would take weeks, and as a consequence, she needed someone to help take care of the plump, new arrival, Mary Elizabeth. With Katie's assistance, Aunt Abigail recovered fully, and little Mary Elizabeth, over the course of six weeks, became even plumper and happier.

Unfortunately, the effects on Mrs. O'Malley were devastating. Her health deteriorated, and she was forced to retreat to her bed. Within an hour of returning to the farm, Katie had donned her special dress and danced. As she finished, she noticed an immediate improvement in her mother, who got up and danced a little jig herself. During this performance, Mr. O'Malley and Finn had walked in from outside, kicking off the tiny amount of snow that had stuck to their boots. Mr. O'Malley had stepped into the downstairs bedroom to secure his rifle in its cabinet, but Katie had noticed Finn waiting in the kitchen, watching her carefully, and then listening just as intently as Katie's mother praised the performance. Finn left a few minutes later. After supper that night, Katie pulled her father aside.

"I don't like this at all. I can tell he's suspicious."

"But all Finn saw was you dancing," her father protested.

"Was it?" asked Katie. She felt he had to have noticed how the appearance of the dress had changed. When her father had hired Finn, it had been a simple, dark costume with a pattern of seven yellow gems on the torso. However, every time Katie danced, the dress changed. The material had grown lighter, both in weight and in appearance, like the first hint of sunlight modifying the inky void of a moonless night. More jewels had appeared too, gradually, forming intricate Celtic designs. Now, months later, the dress was an iridescent green with scores of sparkling gemstones, like starlight reflecting off the crests of waves on an emerald sea. Yet, on the torso, the seven golden stones stood out in their original pattern.

"Look, Katie," said her father, "this man is not very smart. I've seen how he lives. I doubt whether he understands what we have here."

"But," continued Katie, "today he saw how the dress affected mother!"

"He saw how happy it made her," said her father, smiling, attempting to calm his daughter. "But I'll keep an eye on the man. He knows that if he tries anything, he's done here. And he can't afford that." He explained to his daughter Finn's desperate attempts to help his battered sister and her children. This made Katie feel a bit better.

"By the way, Katie," her father continued, "Don't go straying far from the house, especially after dark."

"Is that why you were out today with your gun?" she asked.

Mr. O'Malley nodded, his eyes grave. "It's bad this year. More of them than usual."

There were no large predators in Ireland. At one time, wolves had roamed the island country, but the animals had been hunted to extinction by the start of the 19th century. Occasionally, however, packs of wild dogs would appear in some localities, vicious enough to pull down a deer—or a human. While Ireland's winters were normally rather mild with little snow, there were occasional exceptions—such as the current winner—and this left the wild dogs more desperate for food.

"They've already pulled down two cows," said her father. "And they seem to be getting bolder."

Katie shivered. If there was anything that frightened her more than Finn, it was wild dogs.

# 4

Despite her father's assurances, Katie could not sleep. Finn's dark eyes seemed burned into her mind. What if he tried to steal the dress?

She forced herself to remember her father's assurances. Finn had a family to care for. He could not afford to lose his job.

On the other hand, how much money would a magic dress bring?

As midnight approached, Katie still found herself wide awake. She went to the crack in the wall, knelt, and peered down into the dark kitchen.

*Will they come tonight?*

Her father had left extra honey and milk, as he always did. For awhile, nothing. Then, a slight scampering sound, and the soft glow from the fairies' lantern illuminated the kitchen. The creatures gorged themselves for several minutes at the stone, and then they plunged into their work. Katie smiled, thankful for the help they had rendered while her mother was ill, wishing that she might talk to them. Not that it would do any good. Even if the little beings had not been in the habit of shying away from humans, Katie doubted she would understand much of their strange language.

*But they understand us,* she reminded herself, for they seemed to have overheard Katie and her father talking about dance and her mother's illness.

Then, just moments after the half-dozen had disappeared outside, one of them raced back into the kitchen, chattering frantically. The others instantly ceased their work, the light was doused, and the troupe fled from the kitchen. In the last of the lantern light, Katie saw why.

Finn's face in the tiny window above the kitchen sink.

Now he knew. Even Finn would have certainly made the connection between the magic of the fairies and the magic of the dress. She woke her father and told him immediately. He retrieved his gun, poked around outside. Finn's footprints were indeed in the thin layer of snow beneath the window, after which they led off the property. Mr. O'Malley checked inside the byre and around the stone outbuildings as well. When he had finished, the dress was removed from Katie's room to the chest at the foot of her parents' bed, and Katie slept between her mother and father the remainder of the night.

Finn failed to show up for work the next day.

"I'm not surprised," said Mr. O'Malley. "I suppose we've seen the last of him."

Still, Mr. O'Malley paused in his work frequently throughout the day to look about and listen. And he made certain that his rifle was never more than a few steps away.

That night, the dress remained in the chest at the foot of her parents' bed, though Katie slept in the loft. She had climbed under the covers just after ten o'clock and had lain awake for a quarter hour, worrying a hole into the wooden ceiling above her head, when she detected a soft, golden light through the crack in the wall.

*The fairies!*

Katie bounced up and held her eye to the crevice, but what she saw was not the fairies. Indeed, the kitchen was empty, but yellow light flickered through the window above the sink.

*There's a fire outside!*

She raced down the loft stairs barefoot and burst into her parents' room. "Fire! Fire! Outside!"

Her father bolted up in an instant, pulled on his trousers and shoes, and rushed out the door. Katie followed and stopped at the threshold, leaning into the frigid night. She watched her father in silhouette against the red glow of flames leaping above the thatched roof at the near corner of the byre. He slowed as he approached the structure and called over his shoulder. "Stay in the house! I'm going to turn the herd loose!" While the walls of the byre were stone, the roof was straw — the only roof in their compound that had not been replaced with tin — and the beams were wood. Katie knew the smoke and heat might injure or kill the animals, whose terrified cries issued from within. She could not help but wonder how it had started. As Mr. O'Malley turned back toward the byre, a dark figure darted out from the corner of the house behind him and slammed a broken fence board into the back of his head. Katie watched her father crumple onto the frozen ground. His assailant now stood in the light, his features clear even from a distance.

*Finn!*

The former hired man towered over John O'Malley and brought the board down again on his victim, who lay in the snow unmoving. Finn was about to hit him a third time when something tore into the back of Finn's right leg. A savage pain erupted, forcing him to one knee. He turned to see Katie standing just behind him in her nightgown and bare feet, holding a fireplace poker.

"You leave him alone, Finn! And get off our land!"

Finn's lip curled in anger, and he struggled to a standing position. Then he burst into a grotesque, hobbling sprint, kicking up a thin spray of snow, his dark eyes on Katie. Katie screamed and turned toward the house, but her bare feet had little feeling in them and Finn was much quicker. He grabbed Katie's left wrist, fending off a weak swing of the fireplace poker with his forearm, wresting it from her grip. Then he raised it above his own head, intending to bring it down on the girl struggling at arm's length, when a gunshot echoed through the winter night. Finn released his grip on Katie's wrist, and she pulled farther away from him, straightening. She saw her assailant drop the fireplace poker, which bounced onto the ground next to a fresh spray of blood. Finn doubled over but remained on his feet.

"D-don't shoot!"

Katie turned toward the open doorway to her house. There, on the stoop, stood her mother in her nightgown, holding the rifle that still pointed in Finn's direction. She spoke in a cold, clear voice. "Don't you ever touch my daughter again!"

Katie had never felt so relieved nor so proud of her poor, sick mother. "Mama—" She took a step toward the house, and then stopped as her mother lowered the gun, seemed to sway slightly, catch herself, and then fell sideways off the stoop into the snow.

# 5

Katie ran to her mother, crouched over her, stared into her white face. Her mother's breaths came in short gasps. Her eyes seemed unable to focus.

"Mama!"

She heard a grunt from behind, and Finn pulled her up by the back of her nightgown, dragging her into the house.

"Mama!"

"She shot me!" croaked Finn, tossing the girl into a heap on the wooden kitchen floor. He then retrieved the rifle from where it had fallen near the steps. Katie saw that one hand held his side, the clothes soaked crimson. He pulled open cupboard drawers until he found a dish cloth, which he pressed against the wound. The pain of the simple act made him jerk like a marionette, and he spoke through gritted teeth. "If she doesn't get here soon, I'll bleed to death!"

These words made no sense to Katie. She tried to get up, but Finn kicked her hard in the shoulder with the flat of his boot, knocking the wind out of her.

"Stay where you are!"

"My mama! She needs help!"

"So do I!" growled Finn. An idea seemed to occur to him. "You help me, and I'll help her!"

Katie shook her head. "Help her now! She's sick!"

"You get me that magic dress, I help your mama!" said Finn, wincing.

"No, you can't have it!" cried Katie. "Without it, she'll die!"

"If you don't get it for me, I'll put a bullet in her right now!" roared Finn, whose eyes seemed to be on fire. "I need that dress when the Cailleach gets here!"

"How can you do this to us?" cried Katie bitterly. "My father said you were a good man who was trying to help his family!"

Finn laughed, but only for an instant, for it made him wince. "You mean the woman I showed him? I didn't even know her name! She agreed to let me show off her charming home in exchange for a bottle. Your fool of a father believed what he wanted to believe!"

She knew she had no choice. Katie pulled herself up off the floor, grimacing over the pain from her aching shoulder. She pushed open the slightly ajar door to her parents' room, tears streaming down her cheeks as she approached their empty bed. Her mother lay dying out in the frozen yard. And her father? She could not tell whether Finn had killed or stunned him. Only half an hour ago, both parents had been lying asleep, safe in this very bed. But Finn had robbed them of their happiness, possibly their lives. And he had done it for some woman that would be arriving there tonight.

*If I live through this night, I'll make them pay!*

She opened the chest at the foot of the bed and removed the neatly-folded dress. She could not bear the thought of letting it go. But she had no way to fight Finn. She brought it out into the kitchen. Finn reached out for it, saw the blood on his hand and drew it back.

"Put it in something. A pillowcase." He moved his hand back to where it had been applying pressure to the rag over his wound. Katie noticed that sweat had broken out upon his forehead. She retrieved a pillowcase from the bedroom, neatly folded the dress, and slid it inside. Then she dropped the sack on the floor near Finn's feet.

"Now help my mother!" Katie noticed her own voice shaking.

"I'll help her when the Cailleach gets here," said Finn. "She'll fix me up!"

Katie was about to ask what he meant when the wind swept through the open doorway with renewed intensity. When it died back a few moments later, a woman in a long, white, formless cloak stood in the opening, the flames from the roof of the burning byre creating moving, nightmarish shadows across her face. She might have been one hundred years old, with deep wrinkles, dark eyes set deep into her skull, and long, stringy hair the color of ice. Katie felt a chill that had nothing to do with the temperature.

Finn turned jerkily toward the woman. "Help me! I've done what I promised!"

The old woman smiled, though there was no kindness in it. "So the stories are true! The fairies took pity on a kind family with a sick mother, creating something powerful enough to cheat death…at least for a little while."

"Please!" cried Katie. "Help my mother!"

"Silence, Daughter of Man!" screeched the Cailleach. "Or I'll cast you out to the wild dogs! They are running in great numbers tonight! And they are hungry!"

"Here!" Finn kicked the pillow case toward the doorway. "Now use your magic! Heal me! And then my money!"

The word tumbled out before Katie could stop it. "Magic?"

The Cailleach reached down, picked up the pillowcase. She smiled indulgently, an ugly smile made uglier by a malice that came from deep within. "Are you fool enough to think that the fairies are the only magical creatures, child? They are mere worms compared to those of us who *rule* the realm! Ugly, stupid creatures who could extort a fortune from simple-minded mortals, yet the fairies are content to work like slaves for table scraps. It is true that some of them are clever craftsmen, but even in this, their limited imagination is apparent. Look here!" She raised the pillowcase. "They create a remarkable dress whose energy could change the orbit of the planet if one wished. A dress that could topple kings, alter the course of rivers, lay waste to nations, command a fortune in gold— or render it as worthless as lead. Yet, these dim creatures give this unprecedented gift to *you*, where its effects will create nary a ripple on the surface of the wider world."

"Take the dress!" cried Katie. "I don't care how valuable it is! But if you're a healer, heal my parents first! Then take it and leave!"

The Cailleach scowled at Katie. "I'll do what I wish, Daughter of Man! I can turn the burbling streams of summer into rock-solid ice at a moment's notice! I can gaze across the farmlands and wither every green and growing crop! But...you have given me an idea. There *is* one thing I cannot do. But *you* can! You're young. The dress was made for you. And you have spirit! Yes, you would be an apt conduit!"

"Please!" groaned Finn. "I've done my part!"

The Cailleach gave him a look of utter hatred and continued.

"The fairies were clever in one respect. Only a Daughter of Man can wear the dress. When she dances, the seven golden beryls sewn into the bodice collect energy—which may be directed anywhere! To me, for instance! Yes, you can be my conduit! You will dance, and I will grow more powerful! In return, I will save your parents!"

Katie's heart pounded rapidly. "You'll really do that?"

"You dare doubt my word?"

Katie thought of the empty bed behind her, of her two parents lying in the snow, nearly frozen, perhaps hovering near death. She thought of her mother's poor health. All the damage could be undone. They could be restored to wholeness with a single word.

"Agreed," said Katie. "Now please, help my parents!"

"Patience, wretch," said the Cailleach. "I have not yet inspected my merchandise to see whether Mr. Finn has lived up to his part of the bargain that he made when he sought me out."

"Of course I have!" said Finn with some effort. "I'm no fool!"

The Cailleach pulled out the dress, held it aloft with both hands, smiling. Then, the smile vanished.

"You're no fool?" screeched the Cailleach furiously, turning on the hunched-over man, who staggered and fell to his knees, his free hand raised as if to deflect a blow. "Then why do you try to cheat me?"

"I-I don't understand!" Finn gradually lowered his hand.

"The gems!" hissed the Cailleach. "The seven golden beryls! What have you done with them?"

The old woman held up the dress. Katie hugged herself against the cold and saw that the gems were indeed gone.

"Or was it you?" cackled the crone, turning now on Katie. But then the anger melted out of her expression, replaced by a calculated wariness. "No! It was the fairies! Of course! Our friend, Mr. Finn, must have carelessly revealed himself to them, making them suspicious. They must have hidden them. But I have the resources of the world at my fingertips! I will recover them...and I must start now!"

The old woman turned, dress over a forearm, and stepped onto the stoop.

"But I did what you asked!" shouted Finn, struggling to his feet. "I fulfilled my bargain! I got the dress for you! You owe me!"

At this, the old woman stopped on the stoop, turned and smiled foully. "A mutilated dress. And for this you expect a reward? Very well! Follow me!" The fire had largely died back. The Cailleach stepped slowly into the snow and began walking through the smoky yard toward the meadow to the south. Finn followed.

"Wait!" cried Katie, stepping out onto the cold ground. "My parents!"

"Without the stones, you cannot fulfill your part of our bargain," said the old woman. "And so I have no need to fulfill mine." Then she stopped and turned back toward the girl. "But as I said, you have spirit. And so I will give you a chance. Run! Right now! Don't wait a second! Run for help! It's about two miles. If you make it, I'll protect your parents until you return with help."

"But I've nothing on my feet!"

"This is your chance!" cried the Cailleach, and Katie took off running, her form quickly obscured by the swirling snows and the dark.

The Cailleach turned again to the south. "She will not make it. As I said, the wild dogs are numerous tonight."

They crossed the yard and headed across a meadow, tall grasses pushing through the modest snow cover. Finn struggled to keep up. He noticed he had fallen half a dozen paces behind, and the walking had worsened the bleeding from his side.

"Where are we going? Can't you heal me now?"

"We're almost there, Mr. Finn," said the Cailleach without turning around.

They walked a bit longer in silence before Finn realized he was now twice as far behind.

"I don't even care about the money anymore," said Finn. "I just…every step, it hurts."

The Cailleach continued to walk. "Don't worry. I'm going to take care of you."

He tried to quicken his pace, even though this increased his pain. He focused on the trail the Cailleach left in the new snow, and then, suddenly, he was breaking the trail himself. Looking up, he no longer saw the Cailleach, nor any tracks suggesting where she might have gone. The farmhouse was no longer visible behind and the cold wind tore savagely at him. Oddly, his mind was suddenly clear, completely aware of every sensation.

That was when he heard the frenzied growls of the approaching wild dogs.

# Part II

*New York City*
*One Year Ago*

*Ethan's Tale*

# Crack in the Looking Glass

# 6

Friday. Payday. Ethan would have enough for a few new comic books, for a movie ticket, and to help with the family's groceries. Of course, he would also buy food for the birds.

This last thought brought a smile.

He cut across a side street toward an alley that ran behind the row of nearly identical Staten Island brownstones. Returning from his job at Feldberg's, he had spent twenty minutes on the subway, another twenty-five on the ferry, and now, another fifteen on the walk up from the ferry landing. In a few minutes, he would be on the rooftop, his favorite place in the world.

Ethan had worked at Feldberg's for just over a year, starting shortly after his sixteenth birthday. He could have bagged groceries or washed dishes on the island, but Feldberg's paid a bit better and the ferry was, after all, free. Feldberg's was located in New York's Garment District, a roughly rectangular area covering twenty city blocks in the middle of downtown Manhattan. One could walk along 7th Avenue and marvel at the names of fashion industry leaders, visionaries, and the trendiest designer labels. This—the Garment District—was where it happened. If someone on a television awards show wore a stunningly beautiful dress—or even a stunningly ugly one—it had probably originated here. If fancy-label jeans showed up at an outlet store in Missoula, Montana, a genius in an office in Midtown was probably responsible for how snugly or loosely they fit.

Ethan contributed in less glamorous ways. Feldberg's was a fabric shop and warehouse wedged between other businesses near the north end of the district. Ethan cleaned, fixed, lifted. He was good at the physical labor and dreaded the start of the new school year in two weeks, for this was something he was not good at. His quietness and solitary nature had made it difficult for him to make lasting friendships even in the elementary grades. A blotchy red birthmark that his mother had referred to as a port wine stain discolored his temple and a bit of the brow above his right eye, leading to additional pranks, slanders and cruelties, and driving yet another wedge between Ethan and potential playmates.

In addition, Ethan had no love for math, reading, or anything else in the school curriculum. He would struggle through them, hopefully. Finish his senior year. After that? A mystery. The Navy, perhaps. Or Feldberg might take him on full time. Or something else.

However, such troubling thoughts would fade away when Ethan reached the rooftop and his true friends. He quickened his pace through the alley, then came to an abrupt stop. A sound inside a dumpster had caught his attention. Not that sounds from within dumpsters were uncommon. Usually it simply meant rats, or perhaps someone's cat prowling for leftovers. However, this had been the sound of something big shifting against the metal side, something person-big. And he was almost certain he had heard a muffled voice say "ow" or something of the sort. Ethan stepped up, swung open the lid and poked his nose over the metal lip. Indeed, a person crouched almost directly beneath him, surrounded by refuse and scraps—a woman, or perhaps a girl, for she appeared very young. At first, her eyes seemed afraid, but an instant later, the fear drained away and she whispered a question.

"Is she gone?"

People did not ask Ethan a lot of questions. At Feldberg's, they mostly told him to do things. In school, his teachers had stopped asking him questions after they tired of him responding with a shrug of his shoulders or a mumbled, "Dunno." He had no enduring friendships or groups of pals, partly because this would have required that he initiate a conversation, which was not his forte. He supposed that was why he loved the pigeons so. They did not require him to say anything.

Of course, Ethan could speak when the situation required speaking, and this one certainly seemed to.

"Is who gone?" he mumbled.

"The old woman," said the crouching dumpster girl.

Ethan gave the long alley a good look. "No one here but me."

The crouching dumpster girl seemed unconvinced. "Could you make sure?"

Ethan slowly lowered the lid, which ridiculous with her still inside, and then he walked up the alley half a dozen houses, even passing his own, and back again, checking behind and inside every dumpster along the way. He then retraced his steps in the other direction until he arrived at the point where he had entered the alley. When he finally returned and lifted the lid on the original dumpster, crouching dumpster girl stared up at him as before.

"I'm the only one here. And you."

At this, she began to rise. Ethan helped her out of the olive-colored metal container. Standing next to him, without garbage covering her from the shoulders down, he finally had a chance to assess her. While Ethan was an inch under six feet, he guessed that she was half a foot shorter still. She had dark, curly hair, a thin face, and a nose that seemed to have been broken and not set properly at some earlier point in her life. She also had an inch-long scar along the left side of her chin. Aside from the unfortunate nose and the scar and the impossibly disheveled hair, she was quite pretty, he thought. Her attire included a nicer than expected pair of jeans, a gray Miami Dolphins sweatshirt and a bulging student-size backpack.

"Thank you."

As might be expected, Ethan did not say anything. He did, however, stare at her feet, upon which he noticed she wore powder-blue jogging shoes whose fabric was riddled with holes.

Half a minute elapsed, the silence becoming more awkward with each second. Then the girl backed up a step.

"I've got to go."

This had an unusual effect on Ethan. For the first time, he actually *wanted* to speak to someone, to engage in conversation. But his lack of practice made the whole exercise seem awkward. He had no idea where to begin, yet, he knew he had to begin somewhere, and quickly, for in another few moments, this person would be gone.

"Wait!"

The word had its effect. She had been moving backward, away from him, and now she stopped. Ethan's mind raced. What should he say next?

Finally, a question came to him. "Why were you hiding from the woman?"

The girl looked around the alley, seemed satisfied, and turned back to Ethan. "She came after me like she wanted to hurt me. I don't know who she was. She was old and had really white hair. And a scar above her left eye. And—this is sort of weird—she wore an odd symbol hanging from a silver necklace."

The girl jogged back to the dumpster, scavenged a scrap of cardboard, and sketched a figure with a charcoal pencil she had retrieved from her backpack.

"It's called a triskelion," she told him, and then, noticing the look of astonishment, smiled. "I know this because I work with lots of symbols. I'm an artist." The smile faded. "Well, trying to be. I was checking out a gallery here on Staten Island this morning. That turned out to be a waste of time! But that symbol, it sort of surprised me. It's very old. Worn by witches. It means death."

The woman she had described did not remind Ethan of any of the neighbors. "Why were you in the alley?" He had not meant it to sound like an accusation, and he was relieved to see, by the look on her face, that she did not take it that way.

"Shortcut back to the ferry. I sometimes take shortcuts through alleys. You'd be surprised what people throw out. Some of it can be pretty useful for an artist."

Ethan looked at his own shoes for a moment. Then his head rose slowly. "Do you need me to help you get home?"

A look of unimaginable sadness passed across the girl's face and was gone. "I'm not from around here."

He had guessed that. And by "here" he did not simply mean Staten Island, for her voice lacked the telltale signatures that characterized most New Yorkers.

"I really know the city," said Ethan, his heart pounding. "I can go with you to wherever you live. You know, to make sure you'll be okay."

"Thanks," she continued, beginning to move away again. "But I'm kind of between places."

Ethan felt like some part of him was pulling away with her, creating a hollow space in his chest. He called after her.

"Where?"

She looked at him quizzically.

"Where will you go?"

"Through the looking glass," she replied, smiling slightly as if attempting to make a joke. Then, when only amazement registered on Ethan's face, she added, "The park," and he knew she meant Central Park, more than eight hundred acres of trails, athletic fields, and woods in the center of the city. She would not be the first person to find a secluded location there in which to spend a night— or more. Then she smiled, turned, and began a brisk walk down the alley. When she reached the halfway point, he called after her once more.

"What's your name?"

She stopped, faced him. "Alice." She started to turn away again, but then stopped, pointed to her own face. "*Nevus flammeus!*"

Ethan squinted, confused. "What?"

Alice wiggled the fingers vaguely on the hand near her face. "Your birthmark!"

Ethan felt himself warm, his face reddening.

"It's beautiful!" she called out loudly and, a few moments later, vanished around the corner of the last brownstone.

# 7

Mr. Dunlop, Ethan's father, noticed his son's changed mood that evening. Ethan had always been quiet, perhaps more so than other boys. Now, however, there was something else.

Sadness.

Even caring for the pigeons on the rooftop of the old brownstone did not seem to help.

"Everything okay, Ethan?" his father asked as the boy leaned against the old loft, listening to the hypnotic cooing of the birds.

Ethan nodded unconvincingly.

It was hard for Mr. Dunlop to talk—really talk—with his son. When the boy was upset, it was nearly impossible. Eventually his father patted him on his unruly, tan hair and headed toward the door that led to the stairs. However, Ethan surprised him with a question.

"What does 'through the looking glass' mean?"

This question so surprised Mr. Dunlop that it took him awhile to answer. His son rarely entered into any sort of discussion, and to suddenly have him toss out a question about literature was especially astonishing.

"Er, it can mean a lot of things," said Mr. Dunlop. "If I remember correctly, it's a book title. Or part of one. The full title is…"

He paused to make sure he was remembering it correctly.

*"Through the Looking Glass, and What Alice Found There."*

Even Mr. Dunlop could read the shock on his son's face. "Alice?"

Mr. Dunlop nodded. "The book is a sequel, I believe. To an earlier book called *Alice in Wonderland.* Why do you ask? I think I may have the first book if you'd care to read it."

Ethan shook his head. "I just heard someone use it today, that's all."

Mr. Dunlop suspected there might be more to it than that, but did not say so. "Perhaps this person was trying to mislead you. Through the looking glass can mean that nothing is quite what it seems to be."

Ethan nodded and hugged his father, which indicated to Mr. Dunlop that he was probably done talking. In truth, Mr. Dunlop felt rather invigorated, for it had been one of the most involved discussions he had had with his son in…forever.

For his part, Ethan decided that his father was probably right. Alice—if that was her real name—had no doubt been trying to mislead him by not divulging specifics, though he guessed she really was hiding out in Central Park. She was young, had no place to stay, was an artist…and the weather was still warm.

What would she do in November?

The soft sounds of birds settling in for the night brought him back into the moment. He suddenly noticed the beautiful, starry sky that even the lights of the city could not obscure. He listened to the low cooing for awhile. Altogether, there were six birds, two that were regarded as "show" birds, though they were never shown in any way. Their home was the loft, an old wooden shack with a hinged door for humans, a wide opening on one wall where the birds could come and go, and a rectangular pen of chicken wire with no roof, into which the pigeons could fly. Mr. Dunlop had built it on the flat roof to house his own father's pigeons years ago when the older man had found he could no longer live independently on his farm.

The show birds, Alexis and Tim, came and went as they wished, but they never flew too far. The other four were homing pigeons that could deliver messages, if one wished, across considerable distances. Mr. Dunlop and Ethan had often used Burt and Ariadne to communicate with friends of Mr. Dunlop's. A third pigeon, Bea, was currently being trained by Mr. Dunlop, which sometimes required him to be gone for hours. The fourth, Grace, was a bit of a mystery. Although a homing pigeon, Mr. Dunlop had cautioned Ethan against using her.

"She's a special girl," Ethan's father had told him. "I'll tell you about it—someday. Until then, our job is to protect these poor, delicate creatures."

This made Ethan think about the only book he had every read cover-to-cover. His parents had tried everything they could think of to get him interested in reading, throwing books of every subject matter in his direction. Nothing lit a fire under Ethan until Mr. Dunlop stumbled upon a short volume chronicling the life of Guy Bradley.

Bradley had lived a very brief life, coming into the world in 1870 and exiting it in 1905. What attracted Ethan to his story was that Bradley was a protector.

A protector of birds.

During Bradley's life, poachers snuck into rookeries in Florida and slaughtered millions of birds in their nests, plucking them clean, discarding the naked carcasses to rot, and leaving their young to starve. The feathers were used to decorate women's hats. Per pound, the decorative plumes actually exceeded the value of gold.

Bradley became one of the nation's first game wardens and due to his vigilance and efforts to educate people, made a huge dent in the poaching industry.

Until he was murdered by a poacher at the age of thirty-five.

Still, Ethan had been impressed by Bradley's integrity. In the spirit of Guy Bradley, Ethan had always considered himself the protector of his loft.

Now, suddenly, he felt the need to protect someone else.

After his parents went to bed, Ethan snuck out of the house.

Troubling questions weighed on him during the twenty-minute walk to the ferry from where he lived on Staten Island. Who was this mysterious old woman? Had she really wished to harm Alice? Or was she simply another homeless person whose behavior had frightened Alice? And why was Alice "between places"? She was creative, intelligent. Pretty. What would someone like her be doing in New York without any friends?

He knew the answers to none of these questions. The one thing he did know was that she was frightened and alone. And he could help her.

He was the protector.

The twenty-five minute ferry trip brought new questions. What if it had all been a joke? What if she had made everything up about being an artist and homeless? He had been the butt of jokes in school a few times. Of course, those kids had known him. Why would someone pull a prank on a complete stranger? By the time Ethan stepped onto the subway, his thoughts were so confused that he wanted to scream. When he stepped off at Columbus Circle and stood at the southernmost boundary of Central Park, he merely felt foolish.

There was no way to find Alice in such a huge area. The main loop around the park was more than six miles in length. In addition, there were dozens of secondary roads, bike routes and bridle paths. And it was more than likely that Alice would have found a place to bed down for the night away from the paths. A search for her would be worse than trying to find a needle in a haystack.

He wondered what he had been thinking. Certainly it should have occurred to him earlier that the chances of finding someone who did not wish to be found in an area of eight hundred wooded acres—at night—would be impossible. But then, that had been the problem, hadn't it? He had not been thinking. He had let his emotions get him all worked up. But why?

Of course, he knew the answer immediately.

He cared for this girl.

He knew, then, that he would have to be more cautious. If he were to protect her, he had to think clearly. And his first clear thought of the night was this: *I need to go back home.*

There was nothing he could do tonight. It was already 11:30. Although the park remained open until 1:00 a.m., there was nothing he could accomplish in the dark. He would think of something tomorrow. Perhaps come to the park, give a description of Alice to the pedicab and carriage drivers.

*But what if it's all a big joke?*

No. No one would hide in a dumpster, really scared like that, for a joke. She was homeless and alone.

He was the protector.

Ethan ambled over to one of the map boards that helped tourists navigate the park. He wondered where Alice might be.

An instant later, his eyes grew wide. Street light filtering through the bough of a tree fell on the map, highlighting the Conservancy Water near 74th Street and also illuminating the attraction just north of it.

Alice in Wonderland.

When he had asked where she would go, Alice had said, "Through the looking glass." Had this been a kind of inside joke? Had she actually told him without really telling him?

Ethan took off at a jog, following East Drive through the park. Nearly a mile later, he veered off to the right onto walking trails that took him along the edge of the Conservancy Water. Just to the north of this was a circular plaza featuring a bronze statue of Alice in Wonderland, sitting on a toadstool, surrounded by the Mad Hatter, the White Rabbit and other characters from the story. Ethan faced the attraction, placed his hands on his knees, trying to control his breathing. Then he straightened and walked toward the sculpture, his heart still pounding.

Something moved beneath the toadstool. He stopped for a moment, then approached again, more slowly.

"Don't come any closer!"

He recognized her voice.

"Alice?"

After a pause, he heard more movement. This time, a small, dark-haired figure stood, then took a step out from the statue.

"Actually, the name is Alby."

# 8

Ethan's father was shocked to find his son asleep on the sofa the following morning.

He was even more shocked to learn that Ethan had invited someone else to sleep in his bed. In nearly eighteen years, he had never had a sleepover.

However, the biggest shock of all came when Mrs. Dunlop discovered that the person in her son's bed was a female.

Ethan kept the explanation simple: She was a runaway. Her name was Alby. She needed protection.

Mr. Dunlop knew what he had to do. He would call the appropriate authorities. They would see that Alby was fed, would contact her family. The police would see that no harm came to her.

That all changed once Alby woke.

She told them her story over coffee and toast with strawberry jam. She would turn eighteen next month. Her home was in Iowa (the Dolphins sweatshirt had been purchased at a thrift store—she had never followed the team, but liked dolphins). Her dream was to be an artist, to have her work exhibited in New York galleries. However, she knew that making a living off gallery shows was unlikely, and so she planned to enroll in a two-year commercial art program in order to gain the skills necessary to pay the rent.

"Why come to New York now?" asked Mr. Dunlop. "Wouldn't it be better to stay in Iowa? Wait until you're a little older?"

This brought a rather somber and sometimes emotional discussion of what she had fled in Iowa: an alcoholic mother and an abusive stepfather, things that were difficult to talk about. Alby shuddered at the thought that the authorities might even consider the idea of returning her to them.

"Do you have any siblings?" asked Mrs. Dunlop.

Alby shook her head. "After I left Iowa, I was living with my aunt and her roommate in New York. I work a few hours here and there as a waitress. Not a lot of money, but some. And things were pretty good. But then my aunt took off to Dallas when her boyfriend got a job there. A few days later, her roommate kicked me out."

After a bit of discussion, the elder Dunlops reached a decision: Alby would be eighteen soon. She would be able to legally get housing near her school and begin working on her degree. Until then, she could stay with them.

"As long as Ethan doesn't mind sleeping on the couch for a couple of weeks," said Mrs. Dunlop.

Ethan shook his head enthusiastically, but then felt his cheeks warm in embarrassment.

The remainder of the morning was spent with Mrs. Dunlop helping Alby become familiar with the house and its routines.

"We'll have supper about six," she stated.

Alby thanked Mrs. Dunlop and also explained that the following evening she would not be there for dinner, for she was scheduled to wait tables at the restaurant. "I'll grab something there."

Ethan expressed concern for her safety going to and from work.

"But I travel all over Manhattan," she said kindly. "You can't go with me everywhere!"

That afternoon, Ethan took Alby to the rooftop, introducing each of his pigeons, doing his best to impress her with Grace's mysterious background. "All dad will say is that she's a special girl."

"I can see why you love it up here," said Alby. "Their voices are like primitive poetry. Beautiful and soothing. I could sit here and listen to them forever."

Ethan felt the same way.

Mrs. Dunlop served her special spaghetti and meatballs for supper, and to Ethan's delight, the dish was a huge hit with Alby, who seemed to fit in at the dinner table as if she had always been there. He noticed his mother and father occasionally offering furtive, conspiratorial smiles to him. Normally, this would have bothered and embarrassed him, but tonight, he did not care. It was, he decided, the best night of his life.

After most of the meatballs and spaghetti had disappeared, Mrs. Dunlop brought out dessert—French silk pie, which she admitted she had purchased at the store. Nonetheless, it was delicious.

Mr. Dunlop entertained them with family stories all through dinner. Alby shared a brief story about Christmas before her parents' divorce when she was a very little girl, but otherwise, she added few details about her family.

Then, to Ethan's horror, Mr. Dunlop started on the story about the trip to the campground in Canada when Ethan was ten.

"I don't know how many times we told Ethan, 'Pack your swimsuit.' His mother even made a big sign on a piece of cardboard and taped it on the celing over his bed!"

Alby laughed.

"So the day of the trip arrives. Ethan goes to brush his teeth, and PACK YOUR SWIMSUIT is written on the bathroom mirror in—"

Alby and Mrs. Dunlop continued to laugh. However, Ethan noticed immediately that something was wrong.

"W-was written on the mirror in red—"

He noticed that sweat had broken out on his father's forehead and upper lip, and the color seemed to have gone out of his face. Mr. Dunlop's right hand moved to the center of his chest.

"Oh—"

Ethan stood up. "Mom!"

Now the others noticed as well.

"Bill?"

"Oh!" Mr. Dunlop repeated, his face twisting in pain. He slid off the chair onto the floor.

"Bill!" cried Mrs. Dunlop.

Ethan rushed to his father's side, shouting as he went. "Mom, call 9-1-1! I think dad's having a heart attack!"

# 9

"Gall bladder!" said Mr. Dunlop, rolling his eyes before signing the hospital release forms on Sunday morning that would allow him to go home. "At least that's what they think. All the heart tests came back clean! I'm fit as a fiddle!"

"I don't care," said Mrs. Dunlop. "It's going to be all low fat, low cholesterol at our house from now on. Except for special occasions, that is." She smiled in Alby's direction. Then she returned her gaze to her husband and frowned. "As for you, you gave me a real scare, mister! And I don't want to have to go through that again!"

They arrived home around noon, and Alby suggested to Ethan that they go up to the roof. When they were alone, she hugged him and whimpered softly into his chest.

"I'm so sorry!"

"Why?" asked Ethan.

"My first night in your house and..." She let the sentence stand on its own. "You must think I'm some kind of jinx or human curse."

"You mean because of my dad? No one thinks that." However, he enjoyed the intimate contact and made no move to push her away. "It's just a coincidence, that's all."

They found two plastic deck chairs and sat there most of the afternoon, saying nothing for long stretches, simply drowning in the soothing serenity of pigeon poetry and occasional traffic sounds.

Around four, Alby reluctantly left for work, indicating that she would be back between eleven and midnight. Ethan remained on the rooftop after Alby left, feeling happier than he had in perhaps ever. Eventually, his father came up, poked around to make sure they were alone, and then sat beside his son in the empty plastic deck chair.

"Seeing you with Alby today reminded me that you're almost an adult. Someday, you'll be having a family of your own. And even though the doctors determined that it was only my gallbladder, that painful episode was a wakeup call. It was an unpleasant reminder that your mother and I won't be around forever."

Ethan felt himself redden again. He hoped this was not going to be one of those embarrassing facts of life discussions. His father saw Ethan's face and quickly continued.

"Not that I think you're going to be making any big changes right away! But there are some things you need to know. You're old enough. And that old woman that Alby saw…well, it might be nothing but…"

This was unexpected. Ethan said nothing but waited for his father, who eventually continued.

"What I'm going to tell you will sound fantastic. You may think I've flipped. That they did something to my brain in the hospital." He paused to chuckle softly. "But it's all true. It starts with Grandfather O'Hara."

Grandfather O'Hara, his mother's father, had become ill a couple of years after Ethan and his family had moved into the brownstone. He had passed away a year later.

"You might recall that Grandfather O'Hara was always a very superstitious man. But it appears that in some respects, at least, his superstitions were justified. Try not to laugh."

Ethan could not imagine laughing. His father had never before discussed anything of this nature with him.

"Your grandfather lived on the farm in Gabriels all his life. When he was in his twenties, just after he married your grandmother, a visitor arrived at the farm. The visitor claimed to be a messenger. He asked whether your grandfather would be willing to offer protection."

Ethan felt his heart stutter. He thought of Guy Bradley, of his grandfather, and of himself—all of them, protectors.

"Protection for who?" asked Ethan.

"Not for who," replied Mr. Dunlop. "For what. The visitor produced a golden gem. A yellow beryl. He explained that it had once been part of a set of seven. Together they had been capable of amazing power. They had been given by fairies as a gift to a little girl to help her sick mother. But an evil witch had tried to steal them, intending to harness their power to do terrible things to the world. Fortunately, the fairies retrieved the seven gems before the witch could act, separating the stones and hiding them in seven secret locations throughout the world."

"And—and Grandfather O'Hara's farm was one of the locations?" asked Ethan incredulously.

Mr. Dunlop nodded. "The fairies knew that the witch would try to find the gems. They wanted to make it as difficult as possible. So they were hidden away with trustworthy souls in unremarkable locations on every continent, and then nothing more was said about them.

But your grandfather got old. When he entered the hospice, he passed along the responsibility to us."

Ethan spoke softly, almost inaudibly. "What do we have to do?"

"Nothing, really," said his father. "Unless a second messenger arrives. As I said, there are seven gems. The witch must find them all in order to achieve the power she desires. It stands to reason that, using magic and trickery, she will find some of them. However, if a second messenger arrives, this will mean that the other six gems have been discovered and taken by the witch, and that she is closing in on ours. His arrival will be the signal that we must take action."

Ethan's stomach suddenly felt queasy. "What kind of action?"

"Move the gem to a secret location."

The trip to Grandfather's farm was a six-hour trip through the Adirondacks, Ethan knew. Someone else was living there now.

"But what if the witch gets to the farm before us?" he asked.

"The gem isn't at the farm."

"It's not?"

Mr. Dunlop stood, motioned for his son to follow. He opened the door to the loft and they stepped inside, letting light from the doorway and the pigeon entry provide the illumination they needed. On the walls were a dozen similar platforms formed by nailing foot-long slats of wood into an "L" shape, and then attaching them to the walls so that they looked like upside-down V's. It was upon these that the pigeons roosted.

Mr. Dunlop moved to the lowest roost in the middle of the opposing wall. Taking a screwdriver from his pocket, he removed two screws and then lifted off the roost. Behind it was a small recess in which rested a scrap of cloth. Unfurling this, he held the tiny golden beryl in his hand.

"If the messenger arrives, we must act quickly," whispered his father. "This stone must be placed into a message pouch and affixed to Grace. This is what Grace has been trained for. She will take it far away from here."

"Where?"

"The location is not important," said Ethan's father. "When it arrives, the man there will start the stone on an even more intricate journey, creating a trail that will take many additional years to follow."

He replaced the stone and the perch, and the two exited the loft.

"Sorry to be so melodramatic," said Mr. Dunlop with a smile. "But if anything were to happen to me, well, you need to know what to do. Hopefully the need will never arise, or will be years down the line. I think it's been about seventy years since grandfather received the gem, so I guess we're pretty safe."

"So it's been here ever since Grandfather O'Hara left the farm?"

Mr. Dunlop nodded.

One more question troubled Ethan. "How do you know it's real?"

"You mean the magic?"

Ethan nodded.

Mr. Dunlop sighed. "I asked your grandfather the same question. His own certainty was very convincing. But what really won me over was a little demonstration. He had me put the beryl under my pillow for a night. It gave me a vision of what the world would be like if the witch got her way. That was all I needed to see."

After his father patted him on the shoulder and exited the roof, Ethan knew that sleep would not come easily to him that night, not with the new knowledge he had been given. He also felt the incredible weight upon his shoulders that a protector must feel.

Now he had two things to protect.

His parents retired a bit after ten, and as he sat on the sofa, waiting for Alby to return, he wondered how much he should tell her. He wanted to tell her everything.

But he was a protector. And so he would tell her nothing.

At least for now.

Perhaps there would be a day in the not-too-distant future when it would be appropriate and necessary to tell her the whole story.

As he lost himself in pleasant musings, he heard the rattle of the key in the front door. His mother had given a spare to Alby. In she tumbled, but instead of the look of weary gratitude that he had expected, she wore a look of terror. She pushed herself back against the door and turned the latch. Then she ran to where he stood near the sofa and grabbed his arm.

"It was her again!" said Alby, doing her best to project strength, yet, unable to keep a tear from sliding down her cheek. "She followed me here all the way from the ferry!"

Ethan's throat went dry, but he stepped to the door and peered through the side window.

Nothing.

He checked other windows as well, but saw nothing unusual for 11:30 at night. However, he now knew that Alby's first encounter with the old woman had been no coincidence.

The witch was closing in.

# 10

After Alby fell asleep, Ethan continued to sit on the sofa, thinking.

He knew what he had to do.

Taking a flashlight, he quietly climbed the stairs to the rooftop and eased through the door of the loft. A couple of the birds made soft sounds on their perches, not startled but perhaps curious about his appearance at this late hour. A moment later, he removed the screws, retrieved and pocketed the golden beryl. Then he silently returned to the sofa.

His father had indicated that he would see what the witch was planning if he placed the gem beneath his pillow. He had to see it. He had to know if it was real. Lives depended on him knowing.

Ethan rolled up a t-shirt and set the pumpkin seed-sized stone on top of it so that it would not slip down between the cushions. He placed his pillow on top of the gem and then settled his head onto it.

He exhaled, tried to relax.

Ten minutes passed.

He felt exactly the same.

After awhile, his thoughts inevitably went to Alby. How different their lives were. She had come from a fractured family where being at home meant unthinkable horrors. He, on the other hand, had parents who loved him unconditionally. Then again, she now had her life all planned out. She would get a degree in commercial art and pursue her other artistic passions in her spare time. Ethan had no idea what he wanted to do after high school.

No, that was not completely true.

Since Alby had arrived, he did have *some* idea of what he wanted after graduation. But did *she* want the same thing?

He also thought of how afraid she must be. In an unfamiliar place. No family. In the middle of something so strange and dangerous that she would think he was crazy if he told her the truth.

But he could not tell her the truth.

All he could do was protect her.

And suddenly, he was no longer awake. He stood on the roof of the brownstone, looking out toward the horizon, the sun rising, pouring orange light onto the world. From the rooftop, he gazed down the long street to the Hudson—though no such street allowed such a view in the awake world. As the sun rose, the water shimmered richly, a deep blue.

But then it changed. The waves paled, in seconds going from ultramarine to cerulean to powder blue. Ripples disappeared from the surface. In a few moments, the entire river had frozen solid. The buildings in the background—the familiar Manhattan skyline—developed a crust of ice. Windows shattered as metal frames contracted too quickly. Cars stalled. The hulls of boats crumpled as ice thickened, expanded and exploded upwards. Helicopters plunged from the sky, their rotors snapping off like icicles.

Across the frozen Hudson came a tiny white figure. As the figure reached the island, the ice seemed to follow, like a living, creeping wedding train, covering buildings, killing anything green, first turning leaves and grass brown, then dusting them with frost crystals, paralyzing moving vehicles—and people. The figure came closer, chilling and killing more of the island with each step, and now he could see that it was an ancient, white-haired woman.

And she was laughing.

The laughter echoed off the silent, ice-glazed buildings, shattering more windows and causing some entire structures to crumble as if they had been made of glass. Then the snows swept in, burying buses and cars, pulling down electrical wires, collapsing roofs and bridges. The world was silent now, except for one sound: a thunderous pounding, loud and regular. Ethan realized it was his own heartbeat.

And then he woke.

He felt cold, and it took a few minutes to rub himself warm. Then he retrieved the gem, climbed to the rooftop and replaced it in its hiding place inside the loft.

It was past four before he fell asleep.

When he woke, he felt irritable, and he knew he would never feel normal and happy again unless he found a way to stop the witch.

There were no guns in the house. There were plenty of kitchen knives, but Ethan did not trust himself to use a knife effectively at such close range. If he missed the first time, he might not get a second chance.

Then, in his room, he came upon his old baseball bat. It was a reminder of one shining moment, at age eleven, when he had been the hero for a day—before going back to being a nobody. His parents had signed him up for a youth league team where, despite his muscular frame, he had performed unremarkably. His teammates had mostly tolerated him, though he had earned the nickname

"Mope," which he had hated. Then, in the second-last game of the season, with two men on base and his team one run down against the league-leading Barracudas, Ethan had smashed a home run over the left field chain link fence, and his team had won the game.

He had been mobbed at home plate by joyful teammates, had actually been carried off the field. It had been the only home run he had ever hit. And he had used this exact bat.

Now he would use it again.

Just before 8:00, Ethan called in sick at Feldberg's. He was glad that his parents had already left for their own jobs so that he did not have to explain. He told Alby nothing about the golden beryl or his horrifying vision. When she woke, he could tell she was still shaken by events of the previous night.

"What if she comes after me again?" asked Alby.

"I have a plan," Ethan replied, although he refused to share the exact nature of it with her. "And she's not really after you." He also refused to explain to her how he was certain of this.

"Trust me."

He spent the day on the rooftop, patrolling the edges over and over in an endless rectangle, watching for any sign of the witch on the street or in the back alley. Being three stories up gave him an excellent view of the area for blocks, yet, it was low enough so that he could still identify faces clearly.

Alby came up at three in the afternoon before leaving for the restaurant.

"You're sure she isn't after me?"

Ethan nodded.

Alby gave him a hug. "I can call in sick, too, if you'd like. I'll tell my boss I have the Monday blues. Maybe I can help you here."

Ethan shook his head. "I've got it."

She hugged him and then left.

An hour passed. His parents would be home in another hour. He began to have doubts. What if the witch did not come today? He could not keep calling in sick. What if she could turn invisible and approach the brownstone without being seen? He worried about every imaginable unknown, no matter how unlikely, until his stomach began to churn irritably.

Then, he saw her.

Crossing the street at the end of the block, her long, white hair tossed by the wind. She appeared to be at least seventy, although he wondered whether witch years were the same as human years. She wore black pants and knee-high leather boots beneath an open black coat. While this seemed consistent with the description Alby had given, what confirmed the witch's identity was the sunlight gleaming off the silver triskelion hanging from her neck.

The symbol of death.

He had to act quickly. As she disappeared behind the brownstones at the end of the row on her route to the alley, Ethan clambered down four flights of stairs until he found himself in the cobweb-filled basement of the brownstone. At the back wall was a compartment the size of a small room into which, many years before, coal had been delivered from a truck that would drive through the alley. The space was empty now, except for some boxes of stored items, for the brownstones had converted to natural gas furnaces in the 1960s. The old coal chute was gone as well, but Ethan had left an overturned crate on the floor next to the wall where the chute had once stood. He climbed atop this, carefully pushed open the wooden chute door, and emerged into the alleyway, hidden behind one of the large, olive dumpsters that stood behind each building.

Moments later, he heard the sound of the leather boots on pavement, and the witch came into view. She was walking slowly, as if scouting out the area, close enough now for Ethan to see the scar above her eye.

How he hated her. But in a few moments, everything would be all right. He would be the hero.

He would protect Alby. And the gem. He would save the world.

As the witch scanned the backs of the brownstones, a thin smile fluttered across her face and was gone. She stepped up to the back door of the Dunlops' building. This was his chance, for he was now behind her. He crept out from behind the dumpster, stepped forward quickly, and swung mightily.

The witch collapsed in a heap.

For a moment, he remembered how it had felt to hit the home run. He closed his eyes, savoring it. But he was alone now. And he wasn't finished. He opened the dumpster, picked up the surprisingly light body of the witch, and dropped it inside. Then he secured the metal lid with heavy-duty bungee cords, just to be on the safe side.

He marveled at how easy it had been. The episode made him wonder how the witch had inspired such fear in so many people for such a long time.

He had expected more of a fight.

He had not expected her to be so small and frail.

So much like a regular person.

*Through the looking glass. Nothing is quite what it seems to be.*

He shook off these thoughts. The threat was over. As he walked into the brownstone from the back, he heard the rattle of the front door, and his father appeared, his brow furrowed in minor confusion.

"Home early from Feldberg's?"

"I called in sick," said Ethan, hardly able to contain himself. But before he was able to say any more, his father continued.

"Hey, speaking of sick, I guess it wasn't my gallbladder after all!"

"What?"

"Got a call from the doctor's office today with the rest of my test results. Now they think it might have been food poisoning!"

Ethan blinked. "Food poisoning?"

"Hey, it happens," said Mr. Dunlop with a smile, stepping through the living room and into the kitchen, where he opened the refrigerator and took out a beer. "Funny thing though…"

"What's funny?" asked Ethan, his own stomach beginning to feel more hollow, queasy.

"Well, they said it was strange that I was the only one who got sick. But we all ate the same food, didn't we? But I guess it turned out to be a good thing. Otherwise I might not have told you about our little responsibility." He pointed with his thumb in the direction of the roof.

Ethan recalled his father's words. *'That painful episode was a wakeup call. It was an unpleasant reminder that your mother and I won't be around forever.'* His father had been the only one who got sick. And then he had told Ethan everything about the golden beryl.

"Dad," said Ethan slowly, "you said that a messenger might come."

"Whoa!" said Mr. Dunlop with a chuckle. "What got you thinking about that?"

"How will we know he's the messenger? What will he say?" asked Ethan.

Recognizing that something was troubling his son, Mr. Dunlop now became more serious. "He won't say anything. He'll be wearing a symbol."

Ethan's throat went dry. "What kind of symbol?"

"It's called a triskelion," said Mr. Dunlop. "It's three little spirals." He moved the index finger of the hand that was not holding the beer in a spiral in the air.

Ethan's lower lip began to quiver. "But that's the symbol of death!"

Mr. Dunlop frowned. "No. The triskelion is a Celtic symbol that means to take action. Why, what's going on? Did you see a symbol like that?"

But before his father could finish the sentence, Ethan had turned and dashed to the stairs, taking them two at a time to the second floor, the third floor, and finally, the roof.

*Through the looking glass. Nothing is quite what it seems to be.*

He sprinted across the flat roof to the loft, but now there were no soothing sounds coming from inside. Wrenching open the door, his worst fears were confirmed. The eerily quiet bodies of two birds rested on their roosts while the rest lay motionless on the wooden floor. Tears streamed down Ethan's cheeks as he dug into the hidden recess, but the golden gem was gone. He knew then that she must have only pretended to be asleep, must have discovered the gem's hiding place by secretly following him to the roof last night.

Her disguise—her story—had been so convincing, and now his heart was a wreck. And what of the poor woman in the dumpster? Was she even alive? Would Ethan go to prison? The tears continued to come, but through them, he noticed something else. There were only five bodies.

Grace was missing.

Alby had sent Grace off on her mission, but certainly not with the gem. The special girl was flying to a secret, far away location, to another protector. But why? What sort of payload would the evil witch have sent?

And in an instant, the answer occurred to Ethan. At the dinner table, she had already shown herself to be adept at the art, but this time, it would kill with a touch.

Poison.

# Part III

*Chicago*
*Modern Times*

*Harp's Tale*
# The Woman in White

# 11

The dress caught her eye from across the ballroom. "That's the kind of dress I want!" muttered twelve-year-old Harp McCardle, watching the dark-haired girl awaiting her turn on the stage. Covered with intricate Celtic knots and hundreds of jewels, the solo costume shimmered like a living emerald. Yet, even at a distance, Harp noticed something troubling in the dancer's expression.

*She doesn't look happy.*

"If I had a dress half that nice, I'd never stop smiling," sighed Harp. She had, after all, waited long enough. Eighteen months had slogged past since Harp had moved up to the Novice division in competitive Irish dance, where a first place finish in any of the steps would earn her the right to wear a solo costume instead of the generic dress that displayed her dance school's colors and signaled loudly and clearly to everyone that she was no one special, merely a face in a crowded sea of dancer wannabes. "I'll have my dress in no time!" she had bragged to her friends. But the months of second-, third- and fourth-places had turned into a year. The near misses had dragged on—until just three weeks ago.

Her left hand vibrated, interrupting her thoughts, and Harp swept the phone to within inches of her face.

**WHERE R U?**

Harp's fingers deftly texted a reply to Sammy, her best friend.

**PC STAGE**

Harp's long wait for a gold medal in Novice had not seemed to surprise Sammy, who had earned her own solo dress a year earlier and had already moved from Novice up to the next competitive category: Open Prizewinner. She told Harp simply, "You need to work harder!"

Harp's response was always the same. "I work as hard as anyone else."

That was true as long as "anyone else" meant twelve-year-olds who spent their free time watching television or chatting online—activities that burned few calories and improved endurance negligibly.

Now Harp stood watching the Preliminary Champion—or PC—competition, which was the second-highest division in Irish dance. It was a scene similar to what one might see at any feis, which was the name for an Irish dance competition. The temporary stage was constructed from sheets of plywood only a few inches off the floor of the hotel ballroom. More than a hundred dancers and spectators sat in chairs placed at the front, or stood near the walls along the sides. A fiddler sat at a corner of the stage, ready to play the music which would accompany the competitors. Two dancers moved about the stage, deftly executing their complex routines. Two more waited their turn at the back.

But something was wrong. *Maybe she's sick,* thought Harp, her eyes still fixed on the girl in the gorgeous dress—a dress that did not seem to go with the young dancer's tortured expression. For an instant, the girl's eyes shot across the crowd to the far side of the platform. Harp followed her gaze and then caught herself in mid-gasp as she focused on a tall woman standing out from the colorful throng like a column of ice. The beautiful woman wore a stylish white dress and appeared to be about thirty. But it was her hair that truly captured one's attention: long, straight, and a rich, glossy white—not the dull white of an older person. By contrast, her eyes were dark and liquid— and locked on the girl in the green dress.

*She's probably the girl's dance teacher.*

Mesmerized, Harp drifted toward the stage, felt a bump and realized that Sammy had joined her. Sammy's hair was as blonde and curly as Harp's was inky and straight. Today, of course, both wore the traditional curly wigs worn by the majority of dancers.

"The results won't be posted for awhile," said Sammy, referring to the hard shoe dances they had already finished. "And you've still got to dance your slip jig. So since we have time, let's get some pizza at the food court!"

Harp inched ahead, not really hearing Sammy and forgetting the woman in white for a moment, her eyes fixed on the PC stage. "I want that dress!"

Sammy followed her gaze and stifled a yawn. "Nice. Aren't you hungry?"

Harp found herself within ten feet of the green solo outfit. "You don't understand. You've had *your* solo dress for a year!"

"Actually," said Sammy, "this is my *second* solo dress. But you're right. I don't understand. Why aren't you and your mom looking for a dress right now over at the secondhand rack?"

"Because," replied Harp, "I have to pay for half of it with babysitting money. And that'll take forever!"

Perhaps longer than forever. Her only babysitting job this year had been at the Andersons, and that had only been twice. "She never plays with us!" the children had complained to their parents. "She just keeps clicking!" Then they had made frantic motions on imaginary cell phones with their tiny thumbs.

Mrs. McCardle had eventually offered her daughter a deal: "I might pay for more than half of your solo dress if you'd practice more."

To which Harp had replied: "I might practice more if I had a solo dress."

The two dancers on the PC stage finished and bowed. The girl in the green dress, only moments from taking her place at center stage, seemed a shade paler, her eyes wide as if she were a rabbit surrounded by wolves.

Something's really wrong, thought Harp. "I think she's going to puke!"

Sammy noticed, too. "I think she's going to bolt!"

"Don't be ridiculous," said Harp. "Dancers don't run off in the middle of — "

And before Harp could finish the sentence, the girl in the green dress bolted.

The three judges seated behind a table at the front of the stage looked after her for a moment, and then turned their attention back to the remaining dancer, who wore a flustered expression. All at once, an icy wind swept through the ballroom and the lights blinked off for an instant. As the lights and room temperature returned to normal, some in the crowd shook their heads or craned their necks to peer after Green Dress Girl. An adjudicator cleared her throat, and then the feis continued as if nothing had happened.

"Come on!" cried Harp, giving Sammy's arm a pull.

"Where are we going?" cried Sammy. "And why?"

"We'll see and I don't know," replied Harp, slashing unevenly through the sea of dancers and parents. Part of it she chalked up to simple curiosity. But there was something else. "I think that girl might need help!" She could still see the green dress far ahead.

Sammy struggled to keep up, nearly colliding with a stroller. "Well duh! Like maybe a psychiatric evaluation!"

Harp shook her head. "It was like I could sense something else."

"Now you're a mind reader?"

"There was this lady at the edge of the stage," Harp explained breathlessly as they tiptoed between camp chairs set up on blankets near the far end of the ballroom.

"Probably her dance teacher."

"That's what I thought at first. But when the girl in the green dress looked at her, she freaked."

Sammy finally pulled even with Harp. "When I see one of our teachers and I'm ready to dance, I freak—like I'm going to forget everything."

"She didn't freak like she was nervous," said Harp, trying to find the right words. "It was like if someone pointed a gun at your head!"

They came to a stop, looked around. "Did the lady at the edge of the stage have a gun?" asked Sammy seriously.

Harp answered between noisy breaths. "No."

"Did she do anything more threatening than stand at the edge of the stage?"

Harp shook her head. Then her eyes widened. "She was dressed all in white."

"All in white?" repeated Sammy. Then she raised an index finger while rolling her eyes. "I'll go notify the FBI. Right after I get a slice of pizza." Before Harp could respond, Sammy had disappeared into the crowd.

Whether Sammy believed her or not was irrelevant right now. Harp turned and scanned the camp area, spotting Green Dress Girl almost right away, although by this time, she had changed into street clothes and was zipping up a black garment bag. In a moment, Harp stood behind the girl, who was hurriedly slipping into clogs.

"Excuse me."

Green Dress Girl jumped back and cowered as if ready to be struck. The action was so sudden and the girl's face so full of terror that Harp jumped back a foot as well.

"I was just wondering," Harp continued tentatively, "if you were okay. You ran off."

Green Dress Girl looked around frantically. "Did you feel it? When the lights flickered?"

At first Harp did not understand. Then she remembered the chill wind and nodded.

"She's angry because I ran," said Green Dress Girl.

Harp nodded. "Dance teachers are like that. They think no one should ever get nerv—"

"She's not my teacher," Green Dress Girl said sharply. "I've got to get away now, before she comes."

"I could call one of the feis volunteers to help if you're being harassed," suggested Harp. "Or help you find your parents."

"My parents aren't here, but maybe you *can* help," said Green Dress Girl, "I've got to get the dress out of here. It's dangerous."

Harp's mouth fell open. "You have a dangerous dress?"

Green Dress Girl continued as if Harp had not spoken. "But if I try to leave this ballroom with it, she'll see it."

Harp nodded as if she understood, which was completely untrue. "And then what will happen?"

"Why, it'll be winter for a thousand years!" said Green Dress Girl.

"Ah!" Harp continued to nod. "You didn't fall down during your warm-up, did you? Maybe hit your head?"

"We don't have much time!" Green Dress Girl said desperately. "You have to help me smuggle the dress out!"

"How?" asked Harp. "If I carry it, won't she see that it's with me?"

"You've got to hide it somehow!"

Harp looked at the black dress bag. "It's kind of big, you know. How about if I put your dress on and then put my smock on over the top of it? I could walk out the door and no one would know what dress I was wearing underneath!"

"No!" cried Green Dress Girl as if she had stepped barefoot onto a shard of glass. "Whatever you do, *don't put it on!*"

Harp thought. "I could put your dress bag inside my dress bag!"

Green Dress Girl considered this. "That might work! You can carry your bag out into the lobby and no one will know! I'll come out a couple minutes later, and I won't be carrying anything, so the Kylock will stay in here hunting for the dress, thinking I've left it behind! We'll meet at the fountain near the front desk and then I can get the dress and escape!"

"What's a Kylock?" asked Harp. "Why are we escaping? This is a feis, it's not a maximum security prison."

The look on Green Dress Girl's face communicated such desperation that Harp could not argue. She took the black dress bag and Green Dress Girl rushed off in a different direction.

*This has got to be some sort of reality TV show,* thought Harp. *I'll bet hidden cameras are filming me right now, and when everyone sees this, I'll have to transfer to a school in another state.*

Nevertheless, she headed to her own camp area and slipped the black dress bag inside her own dress bag. Then she slung the strap over her shoulder and headed for the fountain. As Harp neared the doors, she caught sight of the woman in white again, and this sent an electric chill up her spine.

*What if she guesses?*

The woman in white scanned the crowd, probably looking for Green Dress Girl. For an instant, her eyes locked with Harp's.

*She knows!*

But then her gaze moved on, watching others exit the ballroom.

*She looks different,* thought Harp, as she passed through the doors. The woman's long, white hair seemed to have lost some of its luster, and where Harp had guessed her to be about thirty, she now clearly seemed at least ten years older.

*Probably the way the light is hitting her.*

For a moment, Harp considered turning back and approaching the woman in white. Harp felt guilty, putting this person she did not even know through a cat-and-mouse game, worrying her, wasting her time. The poor woman was probably frantic now, wondering whether Green Dress Girl was sick or lost.

However, two things stopped her. First, everything Green Dress Girl had said seemed crazy, nutso. But insane people didn't come to feiseanna—well maybe to judge, but never to dance. In three years, Harp had never met an insane dancer. Not once.

Second, when Harp had locked eyes with the woman in white, she had felt the same chilly wind as when the lights had gone out. Perhaps it had been a coincidence, yet it had been appallingly unsettling.

And so she kept walking, and in another minute, she stood by the fountain in the hotel lobby.

*I hope she gets here soon,* thought Harp, hugging herself to fend off the effects of the chill. *This game isn't fun anymore.*

Several minutes passed. Harp peered around the fountain, but Green Dress Girl was not coming down the hallway leading off the lobby. She waited two more minutes. Then her curiosity got the better of her.

This was her chance to see the gorgeous green dress up close.

Harp unzipped her garment bag and pulled out the black bag inside. After another glance down the hallway, she unzipped this one, too. What she saw surprised her. The green dress seemed much less radiant than it had appeared on stage, almost as if half of the jewels had fallen off. She shook it as if to remove a coating of dust

It's still beautiful, thought Harp. I'd give anything for a dress like this! She checked the hallway a third time. Then she slipped the dress on, just for a moment, just to see what she would look like in a real solo dress.

Mirror panels were built into the lobby walls at intervals, and Harp stepped in front of one. The sight took her breath away. Once again, the dress seemed to generate an electric dazzle, and the jewels sparkled like tiny stars, particularly the seven golden gems in a pattern on the torso. Harp seemed to tingle, which she attributed to the adrenaline rush of seeing herself in the dress of her dreams. And it fit her perfectly, an amazing thing, since Harp recalled that Green Dress Girl was at least four inches taller.

As she stood admiring herself, a familiar voice rang out. "What have you done?"

Green Dress Girl stood a few feet away, her expression now light years beyond terrified.

"I'll take it off," Harp apologized. "It'll only take a second. Then you can have it."

"No!" The girl shook her head. "You don't understand! You've changed everything!"

"You're such a drama queen!" said Harp, slipping out of the dress. "I'll put it in the bag and you can go!"

"I can't take the dress anymore!" cried the girl.

Harp grimaced. "What do you mean?"

"The dress is yours now!" The girl gazed at her sorrowfully, and Harp felt suddenly afraid.

"I can't just take a beautiful dress like this! It must be worth a fortune!"

"You have to take it!" cried the girl, backing away as if Harp had just announced she had the Black Plague. "Now your only hope is to find Brighde before Samhain!"

"Who's Brighde?" Harp called after the retreating girl. "Who's Samhain? Does the dress belong to them?"

"Flee the Kylock!" yelled the girl, and then she disappeared out the doors that led to the street.

Harp placed the green dress back inside the black bag. She zipped this inside her light blue bag and returned to the ballroom. At this point, if Harp had seen the woman in white, she would have walked right up and handed her the green dress. As it was, Harp returned to her own camp, where she related the strange story to Sammy.

"She said the dress was *yours?*" asked Sammy incredulously.

"And shouted a lot of strange words at me," added Harp. "If the strain of being a PC dancer does that to your brain, I'm not sure I want to get that good."

Sammy shook her head. "Well, what are you going to do?"

"I don't know," admitted Harp. Then she remembered her final dance. "But I'll have to figure that out later. I've got to get ready for my slip jig!"

She unzipped her dress bag and removed the black bag. She pulled out her blue Consantoir Academy school dress—and screamed.

"Did you spill something on it?" asked Sammy, staring wide-eyed at the dress held at arm's length by Harp.

"I don't think so," said Harp, her voice trembling, patting the dress. "It's dry."

"It's all discolored like someone spilled bleach or paint," said Sammy. "Oh, Harp, I'm so sorry!"

"My mom's going to kill me!" Harp moaned. "And now I've got nothing to dance in." Then she looked at the black bag. Sammy immediately understood.

"You're not thinking of wearing that weirdo's dress?"

Harp unzipped the black bag. "She said it was mine now."

"She was a psycho!"

"It's only for one dance!" Harp knew Sammy was probably right. The dress wasn't *really* hers. They knew next to nothing about the girl who owned it. But the temptation to wear an actual solo dress in competition . . . well, it was too much to resist.

Once again, the green dress seemed dingy and unimpressive as she pulled it from the bag. When Harp slipped into it, however, it seemed to regain much of its dazzle.

"It looks good on you," Sammy admitted.

"I'll just wear it this once," promised Harp. "Then I'll find a way to give it back."

As she stood with the other twenty girls along the back of stage five, Harp felt a surge of confidence. Not that she had any reason. After all, the slip jig was her worst dance. Harp had not earned better than sixth place finish in the step all year. She knew that her feeling of confidence was completely superficial, due not to any work she had done to improve herself as a dancer, but because she now stood on stage in the most incredible dress she had ever seen.

*Even if I finish last, at least I'll look like a champ!*

And then she was in motion—graceful, high on her toes, holding her leaps . . .

Half an hour later, they stood at the results wall, squinting at the charts and then at each other in disbelief.

"You won the slip jig, Harp!"

She was too stunned to celebrate. "Could this day get any stranger?" Then Harp felt the chill wind, and the lights flickered again. When she turned, the woman in white stood directly behind her, only this time, she looked to have aged thirty years. Harp let out a cry just as the lights cracked and blinked off once more.

When the lights came back on, she was gone.

# 12

Icy blasts tore through her, and Harp McCardle struggled to comprehend the strange, barren world around her.

Two thoughts occurred simultaneously: *I'm freezing* and *I must be going mad!*

One moment she had been standing at the results charts in a nice hotel, celebrating her first-place finish in the slip jig. Then the lights had flickered, a chill had swept through the room, and the lively and colorful world of the feis had disappeared, replaced with the desolate, snow-covered landscape that now stretched to a distant, craggy horizon.

Had she been dressed in an insulated parka and snow pants and been accompanied by a well-stocked dogsled, Harp might have chalked up her confusion to a traumatic brain injury. Perhaps she was part of an Arctic exploration team, had fallen and bashed her forehead against a knot of ice.

But there were no dogs. No sled. And instead of insulated winter gear, Harp stood in this hostile environment wearing the gorgeous green solo dress and her ghillies, her legs bare from the top of her white poodle socks to the elastic edges of her bundies. The curls of her dance wig flailed in the stinging snow propelled by the gale.

A violent shiver shook her, accompanied by another thought: *I'm going to die.*

This notion frightened her, but at the same time, she had difficulty believing it. She thought of her mother, kissing her on the forehead that morning as Harp had hauled her dress bag out the front door toward her friend Sammy's waiting car. "Hope you have a good feis!" her mother had said. How ridiculous it would have sounded if she had added, "Hope you don't freeze to death in an ice desert a thousand miles from the nearest weather station!" Yet that seemed to be precisely the fate that awaited Harp.

Then her father's face popped into her mind, a strange thing, for it seemed to be so warm and alive, yet Harp had never seen him except in photographs. She had been less than a year old when he had died suddenly.

She shivered again, and this seemed to awaken her survival instinct. She was not dead yet. Wrapping her arms around her torso, she shuffled in a tight circle. *How do I get back?* Harp wondered. *There must be a way!* Against the howling storm she cried out, "Hello!" Nothing. "Hello! Is there anyone here?"

And then she saw it. Something moving far off in front of her, at first a mere ripple in the dusky whiteness, but an instant later, closer, definitely someone or some thing approaching.

"Hello!" Harp cried, much louder this time. "Help me!"

The figure moved closer, walking, almost gliding across the frozen land.

"He sees me!" Harp said aloud, almost joyfully, for this surprise seemed to suggest the possibility of rescue. She waved and called out again.

But then she stopped. Despite the terrible, numbing cold, a wary confusion stilled her tongue. Her rescuer was not some scientist studying climate change who had just happened to stumble across a rather badly misplaced twelve-year-old girl in an Irish dance costume. It was a she.

"The woman in white!"

The mysterious woman drew close, clothed no more warmly than Harp, the same white dress she had worn at the feis flowing around her in the bitter winds. But something had clearly altered. Harp previously had noticed a change in the woman's features, which had caused her to appear older. She had initially attributed this to a trick of the light, or perhaps that phenomenon that causes people to sometimes appear younger at a distance than they do up close. At first glance, Harp had guessed the woman's age to be about thirty. As the woman in white approached now through the swirling snow, probably fewer than fifty feet from where Harp stood, she looked to be closer to one hundred and thirty, more like a corpse than a living being. And she seemed to radiate malice, an almost tangible evil that Harp could feel to her bones even more prominently than the chill that clutched at them. The walking corpse drew closer and Harp found herself staring unwillingly into deep, black eyes. Just a few feet away, the woman in white reached out a gristly hand.

But now Harp felt another hand, this one warm and strong and placed on her right shoulder from behind. In the same instant, the blackness returned like the flapping of a raven's wing, and then Harp was back at the feis.

The woman in white was gone.

Dancers milled around the awards area. Most amazingly, no traces of snow remained on her dress, wig or shoes, though she still felt as though she had spent an hour at an ice rink.

She turned quickly to see whose hand rested on her shoulder and found herself face-to-face with a boy about her age. Harp had never seen him before, although he was dressed for dance. He was slim, perhaps a couple of inches taller than Harp, had sandy hair and a spray of freckles across the bridge of his nose. He wore black pants and vest with a green and white striped shirt and an emerald tie underneath.

Harp expected him to ask her if she was all right, to inquire as to whether she might have fainted or had a hallucinogenic reaction to her makeup. She imagined that she had probably been standing there as if in a trance, and this boy had decided to investigate. She knew there was some logical reason for her blackout, and the subsequent dream had probably been inspired by the fantastic story Harp had been told by the previous owner of the green dress.

*"It'll be winter for a thousand years."*

As real as it had all seemed, the odd episode had surely been nothing more than over-active imagination kicked into high gear by the strange events of the feis.

"Are you all right?" asked the boy, just as she had expected, except for a trace of Irish accent. She nodded, although, a bit uncertainly. But then he said something that she had not expected: "Let's get you out of here before she finds you again."

Harp felt her heart sink; her visit back to reality had been shorter than anticipated. She had little time to consider her situation. The boy grabbed her wrist and began pulling her through the crowd. She let herself be led but began interrogating him immediately.

"Who are you?"

"I'm Oen," he replied.

"Where are we going?"

Oen pulled her beside him, released her wrist. "I told you, we've got to get out of here before the Kylock finds you."

The name sent a shiver through Harp, who remembered the girl in the green dress referring to the woman in white by that name. "What's a Kylock?"

Oen turned toward her but kept pushing ahead. "What would you like her to be?"

"I don't understand."

"Do you want me to lie to you and tell you something that you might actually believe?" asked Oen. "Or would you like the truth, which will certainly make you think I'm mental."

"I want life to go back to being normal," said Harp.

"I guess it's the truth then," said Oen. "All right, then. The Kylock is a witch."

Harp stopped, and Oen, after another half step, twisted to a halt as well. "A witch?"

"A powerful one, too," stated Oen. "Come on, now." He turned to continue, but Harp stayed put.

"That's impossible!"

Oen faced her again, clearly impatient. "It's not. You've got legs!"

Harp rolled her eyes. "No, I mean it's not possible that she's a witch!"

"What? You thought they all wore black and rode around on little broomsticks?"

Harp squeezed her fists and eyelids together. "I never thought I'd run into two insane people at a feis in one day!"

Now Oen grabbed her wrist again. "Hurry now! We've got to get you out of that dress!" He pulled her through the door into the great ballroom, but she shook free again.

"You don't get to decide what I do!" cried Harp adamantly. "Besides, I have other dances coming up!"

"You'll have to miss them today!"

Harp took a step backward. "I'm not missing my dances! I'm on a hot streak! I got a first in my slip jig!"

Oen stepped closer and, after missing her wrist, slipped his arm around her waist to usher her forward. "One first is not a streak. And it's not you, it's the bloomin' dress!"

Oen seemed to know where Harp had camped, and as they neared the area, Sammy, Harp's friend, suddenly appeared.  At first, Sammy seemed surprised, then vaguely suspicious.  Finally a smile crept across her face and she leaned in to whisper to Harp.

"Who's the hottie?"

Harp sighed in frustration.  Sammy had completely misinterpreted the situation.  Harp whispered in reply, "He's not a hottie. Well, perhaps he's a little cute, but he's also completely strange and stubborn and even more insane than Psycho Green Dress Girl."

"Right, then," said Oen as they reached Harp's camp. "Pack up your dress. Quickly."

Now Sammy's eyebrows lifted.  "You're not dancing anymore?"

Harp gestured toward Oen. "He says I can't."

"We have to leave the feis," said Oen. "Hurry."

Sammy smiled again. "Swept away from a feis by a boy you just met! How romantic! I'll leave you two alone."

"This isn't romance," cried Harp. "I'm twelve years old! I don't even know what romance is!"

But Sammy had already disappeared into the crowd and Oen continued his explanation.

"The dress is magical. You can't ever wear it around her."

Harp squinted. "Sammy?"

Now Oen rolled his eyes. "The Kylock. She can't talk to you unless you're wearing the dress."

Reluctantly, Harp stepped aside and slipped out of the green dress and packed it into the garment bag. She pulled on a pink I LOVE DANCE t-shirt with the silhouette of a girl executing a leap-over, and light blue sweat pants with the words IRISH DANCE printed down one leg. Under normal circumstances, she would have found an adult feis volunteer and reported the boy's strange behavior. However, the circumstances of this day had been anything but normal. The girl in the green dress had bolted from the Preliminary Champion stage, had asked for Harp's help in smuggling the dress out of the feis, and then had given the beautiful dress to Harp after Harp had tried it on. Harp had experienced some sort of threatening vision involving a one hundred and thirty-year-old woman, a vision that had seemed real, even if being transported to a remote, Arctic wilderness was impossible. And then Oen had showed up to rush her away from some supposed danger.

*Maybe he's not nuts*, she thought. A very small part of her began to wonder whether she might indeed be safer if she listened to him, considering the odd evens of the day. *I'll hang out with him for awhile. And if things get too weird, I can always come back and finish my other dances.*

"Let's go," said Oen as Harp slung the garment bag over her shoulder and picked up her shoe bag in her left hand. They passed through the main door, along the hall and out into the lobby. Oen's eyes seemed to travel everywhere, as if he expected the Kylock to materialize in front of them at any moment. It seemed an eternity before they reached the hotel's front entrance.

Harp pulled up. "Where, exactly, are we going?"

"To find Brighde," said Oen, as if this were the most natural thing in the world.

Harp remembered that the crazy girl had mentioned Brighde, too. And someone called Samhain.

"This Brighde," began Harp, "she can help us?"

"She's the only one who can," said Oen, pulling her toward and through the revolving door.

"And then that creepy woman will stop following me?"

"Absolutely," stated Oen, turning right and hurrying along the sidewalk. "And the world will be saved as well."

Harp shook her head, sighed and trudged along, feeling like a pack horse under the weight of her baggage. "Great. Then let's find her and get this over with."

"That's the stuff," said Oen, smiling as he turned toward her. "So, how much money do you have?"

Harp put on the brakes. "Money?"

Now it was Oen who shook his head in exasperation. "Airline tickets don't grow on trees!"

Harp's eyes popped wide. "Just where do we have to go to find this Brigdhe?"

"I'm not exactly sure," admitted Oen sheepishly. "But I'm thinking Scotland."

"Scotland?" Harp's jaw tightened and her eyes narrowed.

"There are these Islands off the north, the Outer Hebrides," explained Oen. "Actually, their Gaelic name is Na h-Eileanan Siar, and that's where we'll find this holy well—"

But he was talking to the wind, for Harp had spun away and now ran in the opposite direction as fast as a twelve-year-old girl with dance baggage could travel. Her first thought was to duck back inside the hotel, but she did not relish the idea of running into the Kylock or whatever she was. *There are weirdoes everywhere,* she thought, and dashed across the street, stopping to catch her breath between a Mexican restaurant and a coffee shop. She heard Oen shouting as he tried to find an opening in the traffic, but Harp had no intention of slowing down. Five blocks later, she stopped near an auto repair shop, feeling as if she had run a marathon.

"Mom? Come get me," she panted into her cell phone.

After giving directions to the best of her ability, Harp sat on the trunk of an old sedan and stared at the black dress bag. "The sooner I'm rid of you, the better," she said to it, as if it were a living thing. Her eyes darted around the lot. She saw a dumpster beside the garage. With a sigh, Harp hopped off the trunk and walked over to the dumpster. "Good riddance!" Harp lifted the lid and paused. Peering into the dark maw, she heard flies buzzing above bloated black and white plastic bags.

Then she thought about her slip jig. First place.

She closed the dumpster cover. "Maybe I'll wait."

# 13

Harp hardly slept at all that night. With the green dress tucked away beneath her bed, she expected at any minute she might open her eyes to find the woman in white hovering over her. She slept a little better the second night. By the third, she felt certain that she had been overreacting and she slept until noon.

At practice at the Cosantoir Irish Dance Academy on Wednesday, Harp struggled through her drills—as usual. "Girls, you need to make sure you practice on the days you're not with us here at Cosantoir," her teacher, Miss O'Farrell, often said to them. And each time, Harp was certain that Miss O'Farrell's gaze lingered on *her* a bit longer than the others. Harp knew it was true that she did not practice enough, but there was so much to do during the summer: swimming, TV, video games, sleeping late. Today, however, Amy, a girl in her class, said something that no one had ever said to her before.

"Harp, I see you got a first in your slip jig last Saturday! Great job!"

Harp blushed, but the compliment felt good. When she arrived home after practice, she closed the door to her bedroom and pulled the black dress bag out from beneath her bed. She did not open it, but made a decision.

*What harm could there be if I wore it at one more feis?*

She arranged for a ride to the Sterling Feis in mid-July with Sammy's mother. Harp's own mother seemed disappointed when her daughter informed her of her travel arrangements. "I thought I might take you to Sterling myself."

Harp did not want her mother to see her in the green dress. How would she explain it? And how would she explain how her other dress had been ruined? *It was magic, Mom. I'm playing keep-away with a scary woman in white and a boy who wants me to fly to Scotland with him.* Oh yeah, her mother would really understand.

"It's just another feis, Mom," Harp said. "I'll be fine."

The only one who knew everything was Sammy. Harp had expected her friend to laugh or ridicule her. However, Sammy had listened raptly to all the details.

"I think you're doing the right thing by wearing the dress at the Sterling Feis," she had told Harp. "It will help you test the dress. If you have a crummy feis, then you'll know it was all coincidences and imagination."

"And crazy people," Harp had added.

Sammy had nodded. Then she had bit her lip and offered a tentative question. "You don't really believe in all that stuff, do you? I mean, you don't think there's any real magic in that dress? That's the kind of stuff we read about in stories when we were kids. But it's all...made up."

Harp had smiled weakly. "Course not. But, you know, we've still got to test the dress. Just to be sure."

When they arrived at the sports complex in Sterling where the feis was being held, Harp and Sammy set up camp between the two stages upon which they would be dancing, while Sammy's mother shopped the Irish trinket vendors in the entrance hallway. Harp took so long applying makeup that Sammy grew impatient and had already headed off to her stage by the time Harp began to get dressed. She unzipped the garment bag, her hands shaking with nervous anticipation. But then she blinked in disbelief.

The beautiful green dress had changed. This was no trick of the imagination, either. Its sheen seemed to have faded, as if the material was thirty years old, worn and vaguely soiled. Most of the jewels seemed to have disappeared, too, although she could find no trace of them in the bag.

*I'm certainly not going to win any dances in this ugly thing,* thought Harp. However, it was the only dress she had, and so she slipped it on anyway. *Oh well.*

She double-checked the time schedule and headed off toward stage number three. Halfway there, she remembered her competitor number and went back to their camp area. Sammy's mother had returned, carrying a small bag filled with some goodie from the vendors. "What a lovely dress!" she exclaimed as Harp bent to retrieve her number. As she straightened, Harp— surprised by the compliment—looked down at herself and gasped. Most of the jewels in the dress design seemed to have reappeared, and the brilliance of the fabric had somehow been restored. Harp muttered a thank you before resuming her trek to stage three.

She arrived just in time for check-in. The weird metamorphosis of the dress was a puzzle that she would have to solve later. Now, it was time to focus on dance. *I've never been so nervous before a competition,* she thought. But she felt something other than mere nervousness. Once again, she felt confident, powerful.

Before she knew it, she was on the stage, turning, leaping, high on her toes, her movements crisp and precise.

"Four first places!" exclaimed Miss Farrell, her dance teacher, as they stood next to the results posters late in the day. "Harp, you've really stepped it up a notch! I'm proud of you! Congratulations on qualifying for Prizewinner in all of your dances!" She patted Harp on the shoulder and moved off into the crowd.

"That's just plain spooky!" said Sammy after their teacher was out of earshot. "I think you'd better find that dumpster you told me about, but this time, don't chicken out. Toss it in"

Harp beamed at the medals looped around her neck. "Maybe it wasn't the dress."

Sammy scowled. "Harp!"

"Are you saying that I'm not good enough to place first?" asked Harp defensively.

Sammy shook her head as if not believing what she was hearing. "Look, I thought you were crazy for believing that a stupid dress could magically make you a better dancer. I've never believed in the supernatural! When I was six, I set a hidden camera to take video of my parents exchanging the tooth under my pillow for a dollar! But four firsts? In one day? You've never danced that well before! This is a little scary!"

Harp pushed past her friend, heading back to the camp area. "I think you're jealous."

Of course, she knew that Sammy was probably right. Yet, the fact that she had implied that Harp was not deserving of her medals had made Harp angry. Friends were supposed to stand behind each other and be supportive.

But Sammy was right about one thing: This was a little scary.

*I've got to find a way to return this dress to that super-hyper girl. Or maybe Sammy is right, I should just go back to that dumpster.*

On the other hand, how could anyone give up such a treasure? The green dress was beautiful, seeming to increase in dazzle each minute. And in one day it had propelled her from average Novice dancer into Prizewinner status. Were there any limits to its powers? She had to find out.

*I'm going to keep the dress,* she told herself, gaining confidence with every step, thinking of the amazing dancers on the Champs stage. *I'm going to see just how far it will take me.*

# 14

The bony-white hand reached out toward her as she shivered near death in the icy wilderness.

*That really happened, right?* Harp McCardle wondered, lying alone in her room, staring a hole through the ceiling. *The super-hyper girl with the super-powerful dress . . . the hundred-year-old witch . . . the semi-cute, semi-loony boy who wanted her to fly off with him to Scotland . . . I wasn't just dreaming all of that, was I?*

Sometimes, like when she was at the t-shirt shop in the mall with her friends, laughing and horsing around, the memories of Oen and the witch and the psycho girl would pop suddenly into her head. And they would sound silly.

Or she would remember them at dance practice, often as she was stumbling through steps she should have learned months ago—or forgetting to point her toes or not getting her clicks high enough or allowing her arms to bend at the elbows or committing any of the dozens of other Cardinal Sins of Irish Dance. At these frequent moments, the thought that she might possess a magical dress that had guided her to four gold medals in a single feis seemed like the sort of thing one might dream after eating spicy nachos and salsa right before bed.

But all Harp had to do was roll off her bed and pull the bag containing the green dress from beneath it to find proof. When she was alone in her room at home, holding her first-place medals in her hands, it all seemed real and right. *I really won all of my dances! I've moved up to the next level of competition: Prizewinner!*

"It's the dress," her friend Sammy had warned. "It's what is helping you win those medals!"

Harp had nodded. "Because it's beautiful and it's making me more confident!"

Sammy had glowered at her. "Because it's evil! It needs to be destroyed! All of those stories about magical things we read when we were younger. . . just remember that any time someone received a magical gift in those tales, there was a catch or some price to pay. Success— even magical success—isn't going to be free! Remember the story of The Little Mermaid? She was magically given legs, but she had to give up her voice, and every time she danced, it felt like she was walking on knives!"

"Well," Harp had replied haughtily, "what about the story of Cinderella? Except for a minor wardrobe malfunction, everything turned out fine, and she ended up with her Prince Charming!"

Sammy had thrown up her hands and walked away. Despite her friend's misgivings, Harp had ultimately decided it did not matter who was right. After all, if Sammy had found a magic lamp containing a genie who would grant wishes, she certainly would not toss it into a dumpster. No, Sammy would use it to wish for clothes, jewelry, and six or seven new cell phones.

"The dress is like my personal genie," Harp told herself. "Why shouldn't I use it to make my wishes come true?"

And it wasn't like she was using the dress to get candy or toys or other possessions. She was using it to become better at something she loved.

*I'm going to see just how far the green dress can take me!*

Harp had uttered those words less than two weeks earlier. At her Thursday night dance class, however, Harp seemed clumsier than usual, and her only wish was that the practice end quickly. Even though she was not wearing the green dress, her wish came true.

Pop! "Ow!"

Harp slammed onto the wooden dance floor, immediately rolled into a sitting position and put her hands on either side of her right ankle.

"You twisted it a good one," said Miss O'Farrell, kneeling beside Harp. "I'll get some ice."

When she returned with the ice bag, Miss O'Farrell took a closer look at the swollen joint. "Looks like a pretty decent sprain. Keep ice on it and keep it elevated." Then she sent Harp home.

"Too bad," her mother said during the drive. "Looks like you'll have to miss the feis in Gary this Saturday."

The color drained from Harp's face. Miss the Gary Feis? Her first feis in Prizewinner? Even if she placed last in everything, that wasn't going to happen.

*

"You think that the green dress has affected your dancing," said Sammy, dropping her dance bag heavily onto the blanket her mother had spread in one of the few remaining free spaces along the wall. They had just arrived in the wide hallway outside the main ballroom at the Gary Feis. "Not me. I think that dress has affected your brain. You're crazy to try and dance on that grapefruit of an ankle!"

Harp limped to the camp site and unceremoniously deposited herself and her dance bag onto the blanket in one awkward motion. "It's not a grapefruit!" She touched the tender area squeezed inside of her poodle sock. "The swelling has gone down a lot in the past two days. It's more like . . . an orange! Not even an orange . . . a tangelo!"

"A tangelo on steroids!" snorted Sammy. "At the end of the day, it's going to be the size of a watermelon on steroids! Good luck explaining that to your mom!"

Harp ignored her friend, who had already slipped on her dress and jogged off to check the progress on her stage. Sammy's mother offered a smile and then followed in her daughter's wake. Harp scooted across the blanket on her backside, opened the dress bag and removed the green dress. It looked like it might have been purchased at a second-hand store after having previously been used to buff the grime off the exterior of an Army tank. Harp had expected this. Somehow, the dress withered into a bundle of rags in storage, but seemed to blossom into its true, gorgeous form when Harp wore it.

Or—Harp wondered—was the deteriorating bundle of rags its true form?

She laboriously donned the dress, taking an especially long time to zip up the back and position her cape, since Sammy had not returned to help. Then she slid next to her makeup case and performed a few last-minute modifications. Finally she opened her shoe bag and removed her ghillies. Harp slipped off the jogging shoes she had worn to the feis, pulled on the right ghillie and began to tighten the laces so that they would not irritate her damaged ankle.

*There,* she proclaimed as she released the laces. *Doesn't hurt a bit!*

The fact that it did not hurt a bit surprised her. She had expected some irritation, figured she would just have to gut it out. She ran her fingers over the ankle, pulling them away suddenly with a gasp.

*The swelling is gone!*

It was not her imagination. The tangelo was now just an ordinary ankle.

*This dress isn't going to let me fail!* thought Harp, and for the first time, she felt a little afraid of it. However, Sammy arrived at this moment.

"Come on, Harp! Our dance is almost ready to start!"

*

Harp moved across the stage confidently, almost effortlessly. She could feel herself high on her toes, enjoyed the height of her leaps. The music bounced along, and she hit every beat precisely, as if her ghillies could cut diamonds. And her efforts did not go unnoticed by the crowd. Parents whose noses were typically buried in newspapers, novels or feis programs—unless their own children happened to be dancing—seemed unable to take their eyes off of her. Dancers waiting along the back wall lowered their water bottles and paused in their stretching routines to watch the girl in the green dress.

Harp drank in the moment. *This dress is amazing! It's a miracle, not a curse! There's nothing to be afraid of!*

*

Harp had expected Sammy to squeal and hug her after she paraded the trophies for slip jig and treble jig in front of her friend. However, Sammy narrowed her eyes, kept her distance.

"This is wrong, and you know it!"

The comment stunned Harp. "Winning trophies isn't wrong!"

Sammy shook her head and slid away into the crowd. *What's with her?* Harp thought, and was about to take a step after her friend when she heard a voice from behind.

"You danced beautifully today."

Harp turned, smiling, to offer a thank-you, but instantly shrank back with a gasp. The woman in white—youthful, beautiful and smiling—stood just a few feet away.

"I'm sorry if I alarmed you," said the woman in white, smiling gently, sincerely. "I simply wanted to offer my congratulations."

Harp found her breath and, a moment later, her voice. "Oh, I'm fine. I didn't know you were behind me."

The woman in white smiled again. "I'm Mealla," she said, extending her hand, which Harp shook. "You may have seen me watching Kira."

Harp wrinkled her nose. "Kira?"

Mealla laughed lightly, and Harp's tension dissolved. "She's the girl who used to own the green dress."

Now Harp blushed. Did Mealla think she had stolen the dress? Guiltily, she asked, "Are you Kira's dance coach?"

Mealla smiled, putting a hand to her mouth. "Goodness, I'd be a terrible dance coach! I'm like a giraffe on roller skates!"

Harp laughed, and suddenly Kira the Psycho Girl's warnings against talking to the woman in white seemed preposterous, like a nightmare that evaporates in the light of day.

"I'm actually a dress maker," said Mealla. "I made the green dress you're wearing."

Automatically, Harp looked down at herself. "You made this? It's beautiful!" But then she remembered that this dress regenerated itself, healed bruised ankles and propelled average dancers toward stardom.

"But . . . it's . . . it's not normal."

Mealla offered a wry smile. "Are you saying that the dress has some special qualities?"

Harp nodded reluctantly.

"Of course it does!" said Mealla as if this were the most wonderful, natural thing in the world. "There's much that is magical in this world! And there's no more magical place than Ireland, which is where I made this dress! Leprechauns, four-leaf clovers, elves and fairies . . ."

"But," said Harp, lowering her voice, "those are all just make-believe. This dress is *really* magic."

Mealla gazed at Harp with deep understanding. "Some would say we all have magic in us. A great baseball player may channel it through his bat. An archer through his bow. You're channeling yours through this dress."

There seemed to be a certain logic in this, and Harp wanted to believe. She looked down at herself again, suddenly wondering whether Mealla had come to take back the dress.

"Oh, no!" said Mealla breezily, waving a hand at the notion when Harp voiced it. "Kira gave the dress to you. Now it's your responsibility."

"Responsibility?" Harp had never thought of it that way.

"To become a champion!"

Harp smiled nervously, her eyes flitting to the trophies she had just won. "Well, I won all my dances today—"

"I mean to dance on the Champion stage!" said Mealla dramatically, her dark eyes flashing like lightning at midnight. "To be the best of the best!"

Although she had lain awake at night imagining such a future, it had seemed to Harp that no such accomplishments were likely in the real world.

Until now.

"Being on the Champs stage would be so cool," said Harp, turning away from Mealla for a moment, unzipping the back of her dress and slipping it off. "And I *am* dancing pretty well. I might be in PC soon! That's only one step away from Champs!" She slipped the dress into her garment bag and turned back to face Mealla.

The woman in white was gone.

Harp craned her neck to catch a glimpse of Mealla somewhere in the crowd, but she was nowhere to be seen.

*She seemed nice,* Harp thought, settling onto the blanket to undo her shoes. Mealla had gotten pretty excited imagining that the green dress might be worn on the Champs stage, but that was natural. After all, thought Harp, Mealla had made the dress, and she would most certainly want to see it help some deserving dancer succeed. And perhaps Mealla was right. Everyone had magic in them. There was nothing evil about it. And Mealla herself was friendly and beautiful with a charming laugh.

On the other hand, Harp considered it odd that Mealla had disappeared without so much as a goodbye. *She can't talk to you unless you're wearing the dress,* Oen, the odd boy with the Irish accent, had told her shortly after Harp had become the dress's new owner. *Coincidence,* though Harp. But Oen had called her a "witch" too—"the Kylock". And he had mentioned something about the end of the world?

Just silly talk and a hysterical boy who'd probably overdosed on American coffee, thought Harp.

But wait! Hadn't Mealla been one hundred years old? Or had Harp simply imagined this?

Harp pulled on her sweat pants and a t-shirt, and as her head popped through, she was surprised by another visitor styanding directly in front of her.

"Oen!"

He did not look happy. "You talked to her, didn't you?"

Harp had no reason to deny it. In fact, she resented Oen's tone, and so she adopted an air of casual indifference. "So what? She's a lot nicer than you!"

Oen rolled his eyes in frustration. "Look, you can't wear that dress anymore!"

"Because the world will end, right?" asked Harp.

"Right," said Oen. "And you've got to help me find Brighde!"

"In Scotland, right?" asked Harp.

"Possibly," said Oen. "And I should probably tell you that time is running out."

"Of course it is," said Harp. "If we don't find the secret nuclear bomb and disarm it by midnight, the entire world will go kaboom!"

Oen sighed. "If only it were that simple! Look, I can explain on the way! We can get a cab out front that will take us to the airport. Did you bring any money this time?"

Harp shook her head. "You're ridiculous! I'm not going to Scotland with you! I wouldn't even go to the hotel lobby with you!"

Oen's expression seemed defeated, but his eyes darted back and forth as if looking for some way to save the situation. Suddenly, he grabbed Harp's dance bag and took off running toward the exit.

"Hey!" A stab of panic tore through Harp. Now that she had tasted success, she could not bear the thought of losing the green dress. She darted after Oen, zigging around dancers and leaping across blankets and garment bags. She followed him through the hallway and out the front door where he turned sharply left. Harp found Oen stopped on the grass next to a large, funnel-shaped machine that growled so loudly they had to shout to be heard over it.

"I'll give you one last chance," said Oen menacingly. "Come with me and help, or your dress goes into this nasty beast!"

As he pulled the green dress from the garment bag, Harp noticed what the machine was. The landscaping crew that took care of the lawn, pathways and flower beds around the hotel, had apparently been feeding branches and trimmings into the wide mouth of the gas-powered contraption, which then ground it into a coarse mulch that could be spread around the base of the shrubs.

"Don't!" she pleaded.

Oen eyed her hopefully. "Then you'll help?"

Harp reluctantly shook her head. "I can't!"

With a shrug, Oen dropped the dress into the funnel and Harp watched in horror as postage stamp-sized scraps of green fabric sprayed out the opposite end. A cry escaped her lips, all but drowned out by the roar of the machine. Then she turned and trotted back to the hotel, tears streaming.

She knew now that her dreams of being a champion were finished. Back at the camping area, she told Sammy that the green dress had been destroyed. And while Sammy said all the sympathetic things a friend is supposed to say in times of loss, it was clear to Harp that

Sammy felt relieved.  The ride home was silent, exactly the way it should not have been with four trophies sitting beside Harp on the seat.

# 15

Harp wondered how Mealla would react when she learned of the dress's fate.

As Harp trudged into her own house after being dropped off by Sammy's mother, Mrs. McCardle spotted the four trophies from the Gary Feis and gasped. "What a day you must have had! Oh, Harp, I'm so sorry I missed it."

She wanted to say, *Don't worry. There will be other days when I'll be just as successful!* But she knew this was untrue. Without the green dress, she knew she would embarrass herself in her next competition at the Prizewinner level. In fact, as she slogged toward her room, it occurred to her that she might not be able to dance at all in the next competition. When she had become the owner of the green dress, her school dress had deteriorated as if someone had tossed acid onto it. *My dance career is over! I don't have a dress to dance in!*

Or did she? Harp wondered whether her school dress might have been magically restored once the green dress had gone through the mulcher. Perhaps its "spell" was now broken. Harp closed herself into her room and unzipped the garment bag to see, jumping back with a gasp.

The green dress was there, in one piece, looking just as it had when she had packed it away.

Beautiful.

Yet, she had seen it torn to shreds.

If she had possessed any doubts about the dress's magic before, they had now been erased.

*

Harp bounded out of bed early the next morning, completed one hundred sit-ups and fifty pushups, plus twenty minutes of stretching. Then she practiced her dances for an hour.

"What got into you?" asked her bleary-eyed mother as she made coffee while watching her daughter work.

Harp shrugged and continued her dancing, but she knew the answer. It had come to her while staring at her ceiling in bed the previous night.

She had stared for a long time before sleep had arrived.

Winning the trophies had been nice, she had decided, but it somehow did not seem right letting the dress do all the work. In fact, she decided it would be a good idea to work harder so that when she won awards, people who knew her would feel like she deserved them.

In truth, *Harp* wanted to feel like she deserved the awards, too.

As Harp hustled about in practice with uncharacteristic vigor, Miss O'Farrell also noticed her new work ethic.

"All right, Harp! Training like a champ! Good for you!"

Sammy simply rolled her eyes.

*

"The temperature outside must be ninety-five!" groaned Sammy as they unpacked their gear at the Rockford Feis in mid-August. "I'm glad we're inside where it's air conditioned!"

Harp hoped that her friend would wander off to check on the schedule at her stage or to use the restroom or to buy a giant pretzel from the food vendors—anything so that she would not see Harp change into the green dress. On the other hand, Sammy would certainly see it before the first dance, so did it really matter? Still, it would be awkward, since she had not told Sammy the whole story about the dress somehow reassembling itself from a tornado of green scraps.

"Hey, you told me it was destroyed!" said Sammy, wide-eyed, and then frowning as Harp removed the green dress from the garment bag. "I was actually feeling sorry for you! Now I find out that you're just a big liar!"

"I wasn't lying!" shouted Harp. "You can't kill this thing!"

She looked around and noticed everyone in the area seemed to be listening to her. Blushing, Harp knelt on the blanket and began to ready herself for competition. Sammy quickly and silently donned her dress and then disappeared.

Harp tried to concentrate on her makeup. *Jealous.*

Although Harp felt angry, a part of her ached. She and Sammy had never fought like this before. Was discord an inevitable outcome of owning the dress?

\*

Once again, everyone seemed to be watching the girl in the green dress. Harp felt light, strong, as if she were music incarnate. As she finished her last dance and bowed to the judge, she caught sight of Mealla far out in the crowd, nodding, smiling. Half an hour later, she saw her name and number in the first-place box for all four dances in which she had competed. Another clean sweep.

As she read the results, a chill breeze seemed to sweep through the hall and the lights flickered for just an instant. She closed her eyes involuntarily and imagined the barren winter desert into which she had been plunged weeks earlier. Then she forced her eyes open and hurried back to the blanket, where Sammy was already packing. Her friend said nothing as they squished clothing articles into their bags, folded the blanket and headed for the lobby. Miss O'Farrell caught up with them there. After offering a perfunctory "good job" to Sammy, Miss O'Farrell directed her attention to Harp.

"You've really improved, Harp," said her teacher. "It's obvious you've become a very dedicated dancer."

Somehow Miss O'Farrell did not notice the choking noise Sammy made.

"You've got two firsts in each of your required dances in Prizewinner," said Miss O'Farrell. "And it's clear that you're ready for the next level. So at your next feis, you can move up to Preliminary Champion. Congratulations!"

She gave Harp a hug and disappeared into the crowd, which seemed to be rapidly filling the hotel lobby behind them. Sammy spun hard on her heel, turned her face away from Harp and headed briskly across the lobby toward the front doors. Harp followed, pushing through a mass of bodies that seemed to become denser as they neared the windows.

Why are there so many people out here in the lobby? Harp wondered. And then it occurred to her that they seemed to be watching something through the windows the overlooked the hotel courtyard and street. The two girls continued through the revolving front door and finally emerged onto the sidewalk, where Sammy slid to a halt and shouted, "This is nuts!"

Harp intentionally bumped into her friend and sarcastically replied, "Oh, does this mean we're talking?"

Sammy surveyed the scene in front of her. "I hope this means we're dreaming!"

Now Harp peered around her. She felt the chill air. Hadn't it been ninety-five when they had gone inside? Now, however, several inches of snow covered the ground and more plummeted from the sky as lightning tore across the heavens.

And from someplace far off—or perhaps right over her shoulder—Harp heard laughter.

# 16

A mile below, the sun occasionally glinted off ripples that raced across the blue-gray waters of the Atlantic. Wisps of low cloud occasionally obscured the view. Wind whistled outside the cabin of the tiny airplane. That was the most frightening thing. Harp had flown in a small plane once before. Two years ago when a co-worker of Mrs. McCardle's had flown Harp and her mother to Bloomington to see Grandpa and Grandma McCardle. The trip had been full of new experiences and adventures. Mrs. McCardle had pointed out the tiny cars, the ant-like people, and eventually their house. But the engine sounds had required her to talk loudly in order for Harp to hear. Today, there were no engine sounds.

The engine, in fact, was not running.

Harp McCardle sat in the front passenger seat and forced herself to look through the windshield at the propeller, which was behaving exactly the way a propeller should not when one is in a plane a mile above the ocean. The blade seemed frozen at a slight angle. Incredibly, it had not moved one bit during the twenty hours they had been in the air, not even during take-off.

Yet, they were still aloft, cruising along as if everything were normal. That was good. But how long would that continue? Harp wished she had never left the feis in Milwaukee. She would have been back home many hours ago. Instead, she was stuck in a plane no larger than a flying closet that was somehow whizzing along with no visible power source.

And to make matters worse, the pilot was a twelve-year-old boy.

"Only a couple of hours to go!" said Oen, his eyes red with dark circles beneath. "Why don't you sing a song or something to keep me awake?"

"I can't sing," said Harp defensively. "Why don't you just take a nap?"

"I have to stay awake," said Oen, "or the plane will crash. I can only keep it in the air while I'm conscious."

Harp's mouth dropped open and her eyes widened, but she managed to control herself before speaking. "Why didn't you think of this before we took off? Can't you make the plane go any faster?"

"This isn't a jet," said Oen. "It's not designed to break the sound barrier. If I try to make it go too fast, it'll break apart."

Harp considered the matter. It was bad enough to learn that the annoying boy who was trying to destroy your dance career had magical powers. It was worse to learn that there were limits to those powers when their lives were on the line. "You said it's about two hours until we get there?"

Oen sighed wearily and nodded.

Harp stared at the waves far below for a moment, then straightened herself and began to sing. "Row, row, row your boat, gently down the stream . . ."

Oen smiled appreciatively. But Harp could tell that he was tired.

Far too tired.

"Can't you cast a spell to keep yourself awake?" asked Harp, pausing in mid-verse, trying not to sound desperate.

"There are limits to magical powers, you know, especially for kids," said Oen indignantly. "I'm using everything I've got to keep us from going for a long swim!"

She resumed singing, this time more vigorously. *I should never have let him talk me into this,* she thought, recalling the events of the past few days that had brought her to within two hours of the western coast of Scotland.

*

*I'm in PC! I'm in PC!*

The words replayed themselves in her head as she danced her hornpipe steps with the other girls in her dance class. Even though she had dreamed of reaching the PC level for years, the thought brought her little joy, for it was almost always followed by:

*And now I'm going to destroy the world!*

She squeezed her eyes shut in an effort to force this second notion from her mind. It was that stupid Oen's fault. How could a twelve-year-old boy be so annoying? And so tragically warped. He had planted the idea in her head that a witch was using the magical power of her dress to doom the planet.

"All right!" called Miss O'Farrell, her dance teacher. "Let's try it again from the beginning! Now everyone, up on those toes! Ready?"

The music began again, and Harp exploded into motion.

*There's no way my beautiful green dress could hurt anyone!* Harp told herself, breathing hard, struggling to keep going. *Oen is just a big jerk! I'm in PC! I'm in PC!*

But disturbing images swirled at the margins of her consciousness. Like how impossibly old Mealla—the supposed witch—had looked in Harp's dream. Or how the green dress had repaired itself after Oen had thrown it into the mulching machine. Or how it had been ninety-five degrees last weekend in Rockford, Illinois, and a blizzard had shocked the city moments after Harp learned she had won all of her dances. Fortunately, the sun had returned a few minutes later, melting everything almost as quickly as it had fallen. But if Oen was lying to her, what was the real explanation for all the craziness?

"Very good!" called Miss O'Farrell as the music ended. "We'll see you next time!"

While most of the girls shuffled to their shoe bags to change, Harp dropped to the floor where she began sit-ups.

Miss O'Farrell smiled and shook her head as she passed. "Harp, you have become one of the most dedicated dancers I've ever seen!"

Hearing this, Harp's friend, Sammy, offered up a murderous glare. She knew that Harp was getting an assist from the green dress, and felt that nothing except evil and woe would come from it. The two had not spoken since the Rockford Feis.

*What if the dress really is evil?* Harp had asked herself many times in the past few weeks. But then she would remember the feeling of triumph and exhilaration that came with winning her dances, how proud she felt walking back from the awards area, her arms full of trophies, other dancers staring enviously. She had been one of those "other" dancers not long ago, imagining what it would feel like to be *that* girl, the one who seemed to win everything. She liked the feeling. *I can't go back to being a nobody!*

"Some would say we all have magic in us," the beautiful Mealla had told Harp. "A great baseball player may channel it through his bat. An archer through his bow. You're channeling yours through this dress."

Harp rolled onto her stomach and began push-ups. Mealla had not really been one hundred years old. It had probably been the lights playing tricks. Hadn't they been flickering on and off that day? And Oen must have dropped the green dress behind the mulching machine in order to frighten her, replacing it in her dance bag before she returned to her camp. As for the freak snowstorm, there were probably dozens of explanations for it that a scientist might have given her. She had heard so much about global climate change in school. Wasn't that supposed to create bizarre weather phenomena? Harp chuckled at how she had let her imagination lead her to impossible conclusions, switching to a sitting position to do stretching exercises. Mealla obviously did not mean *real* magic. She had most certainly been speaking figuratively, talking about the kinds of special qualities that everyone has inside. *I've just got to work hard enough to help it come out! It's not really the dress.*

\*

Sammy had refused to give Harp a ride to the feis in Milwaukee. As long as Harp planned to wear the green dress, Sammy wanted nothing to do with her.

Harp's mother had been busy, too. "I'm way behind at work, dear. Can't you get one of your friends at dance to give you a ride?"

The Mundanes had finally agreed, but it was an unpleasant trip. Mrs. Mundane drove the tiny car and kept the radio tuned to a station that never played a single song. Mr. Mundane, an enormous man, slouched in the front passenger seat snoring so loudly that Harp was certain she saw truck drivers wince as they passed the

Mundane car. The Mundane siblings, one of each gender, sat on opposite sides of the backseat, wordlessly thumbing away at portable gaming devices, leaving Harp jammed in the middle.

At the feis, Harp realized how alone she really felt without Sammy. She had forgotten to bring a blanket or chair, and so she set up next to a wall in the ballroom where her dances would be held.

Her first feis as a PC dancer!

Normally this would have been an occasion to celebrate, but Harp felt little joy. Her mother was not there to witness the event. Sammy would be dancing on a different stage in a different room. As Harp slipped into the green dress, she felt empty, realizing she had no one with which to share her big moment.

"Are you ready?"

The voice surprised her and yet, it did not. Harp turned to find Mealla standing there in her usual white dress, smiling radiantly.

"I think so."

Mealla helped her to adjust the cape and wig. "You look wonderful! Those other girls don't stand a chance!"

Harp smiled but remained uncertain. "Miss O'Farrell said the competition really gets tough in PC. She said it can take awhile before you start placing."

Mealla laughed lightly. "You're going to surprise everyone, I just know it. In this dress, you can't fail!" Her eyes flashed like opals and Harp felt a very slight chill breeze.

"I'll do my best," said Harp weakly and shuffled off toward the stage.

Halfway there, she felt a tug on her arm and turned as Oen pulled her toward the side of the room.

"Let me go!" hissed Harp. "I ought to scream for the police right now after what you did to my dress!"

"It doesn't look any worse for wear," said Oen, taking a step back. "Do you see now how powerful it is? And you've got to stop talking to the Kylock! She's just sinking her talons deeper and deeper into your soul!"

"Excuse me!" said Harp, pointing her nose toward the stage and attempting to push past Oen. "But I've got to dance in a few minutes!"

"Don't do it!" warned Oen, lifting an arm to stop her. "Each time you succeed, you increase the Kylock's power!"

Harp swatted at his arm. "Stop it! She's not a Kylock or whatever you call it! She's a dress maker, and she just wants to see her creation on the championship stage!"

Oen nodded warily. "Is that what she told you? Well, she's not a dress maker." From his pocket he pulled a page torn from a book, showing the illustration of a grotesque witch above the word "Cailleach".

"It's pronounced KYLOCK," he explained. "Irish folklore is full of stories about her. When she's kept under control, she helps with the change of the seasons and so forth. But she's full of malice and mischief and can do nasty things with the weather."

"Like snow in August?" asked Harp.

"Exactly. She's no dress maker. Your dress was made by fairies and was meant to do great good. But the Kylock is thinking only of power and domination. Did you notice that each time you win at a feis, she grows younger?"

Harp had noticed. "I thought it was my imagination."

"If you keep winning, she'll become unstoppable," said Oen.

"And destroy the world?"

Oen hesitated. "In a manner of speaking. She'll plunge it into a 1000-year ice age. That should take care of most of us."

Harp shivered. The previous owner of the green dress had mentioned this. Then she blinked, looked around the room. This was not some fantasy world. This was a feis in Milwaukee. There were people munching on soft pretzels and bagels, young girls applying makeup, mothers admonishing their daughters for not taking care of their wigs properly. And somewhere the Mundane children were wearing out their thumbs on tiny game system keyboards. This was not Narnia or Hogwarts or Oz. This was Wisconsin.

Harp shook her head. "I still can't believe it."

Oen thought for a moment and an idea seemed to come to him. "If you win today, will that be proof enough? Will you come with me?"

Harp laughed. "To Scotland?" Oen had implored her to accompany him there in their previous meetings. The sincerity in his face made her laugh again. There were twenty-nine girls in her competition. Since it was Harp's first PC feis ever, the chances of her finishing in the top half would be slim. And even if she did somehow win and was forced to finally acknowledge the power possessed by the dress, how did Oen propose to get them to Scotland?

"How much money do you have?" she asked.

The question seemed to puzzle Oen, but he replied matter-of-factly, "None."

Harp had only twenty dollars that her mother had given her for lunch. They would need far more that twenty dollars to get even a single person a flight to Scotland. No matter how low or high she placed today, Oen had no chance of collecting on his bet.

"Deal!"

*

In dreams, one occasionally gets the sensation of falling. And more often than not, this sensation wakes the dreamer, who realizes that she is not falling at all, but rather is home safe in bed. On this particular occasion, Harp dreamed that she was falling, and this sensation did indeed cause her to wake. However, rather than finding herself home in bed, or safe, she found that she was actually falling while strapped into a small aircraft screaming toward the whitecapped surface of the Atlantic Ocean.

"Oen! Wake up!"

The boy's eyes blinked open, and it took him a moment to comprehend the danger. Then he pulled back on the yoke, which immediately had no effect whatsoever. Then the plane began to shudder as if it might shake to pieces. Oen eased up on the yoke and the vibrations diminished but did not stop. After a moment he pulled back again. The plane shook, but not as violently, and in a few seconds, the horizon appeared.

Oen breathed a relieved sigh and smiled at Harp. "Guess I must have dozed off."

"You think?" Harp glared at him. "Why didn't you just put it on auto pilot?"

"The plane has to be powering itself for auto pilot to work," said Oen. "If I fall asleep, there's no power."

Harp could hardly speak. Her heart pounded wildly. "You could have killed us both!"

Oen regarded her with amusement. "Weren't you supposed to be singing to keep me awake?"

She sighed. "Okay, we both fell asleep. But you won't have to worry about me doing that again. I've got so much adrenaline pumping through my veins that I probably won't sleep for a week!"

Harp was not so sure. Her heart was still pounding, and in order to help keep Oen awake, she decided to keep him talking.

"Tell me about the dress. Where it really came from."

"We're not that far from where it really came from," said Oen. "Some fairies took pity on a little girl whose mother was dying. The girl loved to dance, and her mother loved watching her. So the little creatures sewed a dress for her to wear while she danced."

Harp blinked. "That's it?"

Oen shook his head. "They sewed seven golden gems—golden beryls—onto the dress. When the girl danced, they generated energy that helped the mother. The dress changed, too, becoming more beautiful and ornate as its power increased. You may also have noticed that it loses a bit of its luster when neglected."

Harp nodded.

"A hired man on the farm learned of the dress's properties and attempted to sell it to the Cailleach, realizing it was worth a fortune," continued Oen. "However, by the time the Cailleach arrived to seal the deal, the fairies had removed the gems from the dress and hidden them around the world, one on each continent. It took the Cailleach decades to track them all down. She discovered the final beryl only last year. Now she's gaining power. Each time a dancer wearing the dress wins a competition, the strength of her magic increases. Once that dancer completes the cycle—by winning a Champion competition—the Cailleach will have the power she needs to plunge the world into a one thousand-year ice age."

"Why does she want to do that?"

"It's what witches do," Oen said with a smile. "Seriously, though, winter is her time of the year. When it's warm, she's nothing. And she knows that silly mortals are easier to control when they're cold, weak and frightened."

They hit an air pocket, which made Harp gasp loudly, but Oen kept a firm grip on the yoke.

"Why doesn't the Cailleach just wear the dress and do the dancing herself?" asked Harp.

"That's just the way the fairies designed it," said Oen with a shrug. "I guess they didn't want anyone to use the power for themselves. The dress can only be a conduit to transfer power to someone else."

Suddenly, Oen turned and smiled at Harp. "You're trying to keep me gabbing so I won't fall asleep!"

"Uh, yeah!" said Harp, as if this were the most obvious observation that anyone had ever made.

"I don't think you need worry that I'll fall asleep again," said Oen, who then pointed ahead of them. "Look!"

It appeared as though someone had sprinkled a gritty rim along part of the horizon.

"Welcome to Scotland!" said Oen.

# 17

A part of Harp felt relieved, yet another part felt more apprehensive than ever. They had made it to Scotland in a plane powered by a sleep-deprived, twelve-year-old Celtic deity. The fate of the world rested on their shoulders. What would they find when they landed? Would it really help them to defeat the Cailleach? Did Harp really *want* to defeat the Cailleach, considering how well she was performing in dance competitions? And most importantly, how would she explain all of this to her mother?

*She probably has every police officer in Illinois and Wisconsin searching for me by now.* Then she smiled to herself. *Bet none of them are looking in Scotland.*

The feis had ended almost twenty-four hours earlier. She knew her mother was beyond frantic by this time. Harp pulled her cell phone from a pocket and turned it on. Twenty-three missed calls. Twenty of these were from her mother. Harp had intentionally switched off the phone, for she had no idea what she might say. Perhaps not something like, "Hi, Mom. I'm flying to Scotland with a twelve-year-old boy with magical powers. Be home later."

The other three calls, surprisingly, were from Sammy. She pressed her friend's number and Sammy picked up almost instantly.

"Geez, Harp, where are you? Everyone is going crazy looking for you!"

Harp almost felt like crying. Perhaps her emotions were all messed up from lack of sleep. Or from the drama of having almost plummeted into the sea. Or, most likely, she felt a sense of gratitude, knowing that Sammy still cared.

"Sammy, listen to me! Tell my mother I'm okay and that I'll be home as soon as I can. Tell her not to worry and that I know I'll be grounded." In fact, being grounded sounded absolutely wonderful to Harp at that moment.

"But what's happening?" asked Sammy, a hint of fear in her voice. "Are you in trouble?"

Harp took a deep breath, watching the dark band along the horizon thicken. "You're not going to believe this. And you can't tell anyone. Promise?"

Sammy promised. Reluctantly.

"I'm in a plane and we're almost to Scotland. It's actually . . . beautiful!"

She explained what had happened at the feis, including her deal with Oen and how he was keeping the plane aloft with some sort of spell. "After I danced, we went to a small airport just a couple blocks from the feis. There were a bunch of private planes sitting near some buildings and Oen found one that was unlocked."

"If he's got magical powers," said Sammy, "why didn't he just teleport both of you to Scotland with an 'abracadabra'?"

"Oen told me he's not old enough to have that kind of power," explained Harp. "He couldn't transport himself, much less the two of us."

"So what are you looking for in Scotland?" asked Sammy.

"I'm not sure," said Harp. "Someone named Brigdhe, I think. She's going to help us defeat the woman in white."

Sammy cheered so loudly it hurt Harp's ear. "I knew it! I knew you'd come to your senses!"

After a drawn-out and teary goodbye, Harp wondered whether most people would agree with Sammy that her current situation could be described as "coming to her senses".

*

Oen landed the plane in a field without killing them. "I'd actually never flown a real plane before," he told Harp. "All those hours of playing video games really paid off!"

Harp smiled weakly. The first hour of their flight, during which Oen had experimented with the flaps and rudder and other controls had seemed like a bad ride on the world's largest roller coaster.

As they exited the plane, Harp judged that the sun hung an hour or two above the horizon. She turned to Oen who seemed small and even younger than twelve now that he was not at the controls. How had this freckled-faced boy managed to bring them across an ocean — alive?

"You look like a boy, but you're magic," she said to him as he stood illuminated by the late-afternoon sun. "You know impossible things. What are you?"

"Bursting," he said, smiling, and then he dashed into some nearby brush. After a moment, Harp disappeared behind a different clump.

Minutes later they emerged from their cover. "That's better," said Oen. "Now I'm simply starving and tired. But that will have to wait." He made a motion with his hand and they walked over a low hill that offered a view of a strikingly beautiful valley, dropping away to a village in the distance. A bit closer stood what appeared to be a castle, for Harp noticed battlements on the highest tower.

"It's actually a monastery," explained Oen. "But we're looking for what's behind the monastery."

What was behind the monastery at least a hundred meters was the crumbling remains of an ancient well. Oen edged next to the rocky rim and peered into its depths. A short distance from the well stood a scraggly-looking tree with a couple of low-hanging branches. Oen removed his right shoe, then removed his sock and, after slipping back into the shoe, strode purposefully to the tree. He proceeded to tie the sock around one of the low-hanging branches.

"What are you doing?" asked Harp.

"I think it's rather obvious," said Oen. "This is a sock. That's a tree. I'm typing the one to the other."

Harp shot him a nasty look. "But why?"

Oen pointed at the sock. "I'm making a clootie." When he saw the twisted look of incomprehension on her face, he continued. "It's part of the ritual. We tie a piece of clothing around a tree near one of Brigdhe's wells."

Oen crossed his arms and admired the hanging sock for a moment, but then his eyes widened and he stepped up to undo the knot. "My goodness, I almost forgot!" Setting the sock on the grass, Oen lowered a wooden bucket on a rope into the well, and then brought it back up a minute later, brimming with water. He dipped the sock, retied it around the branch, and then stood back to admire his work.

Harp watched the sock, which proceeded to do nothing at all. "So now what happens?"

Oen shrugged. "I don't know."

Harp's eyes widened. "You don't know? You don't *know*? You basically kidnap me, steal a plane, almost crash us both into the ocean and bring me all the way to Scotland, and you don't know what's going to happen?"

Oen grinned weakly. "You've got to understand, I've never done this before, either."

Harp was about to speak again, to let loose with every nasty thing she could think of, to let Oen know in no uncertain terms what she thought of him, his crazy crusade and his ancestry. However, the sunlight seemed to flicker, as if some giant bird had passed overhead. Harp just managed to catch a glimpse of Oen's horror-stricken face before the darkness returned again—and this time it was total.

The blackout seemed to last mere seconds. Suddenly, she found her eyes flickering open again. Oen and the well were gone, as was the monastery behind. Gone, too, were the green meadows.

She blinked, unbelieving, certain that she must be seeing things, but the view remained the same.

Three judges stared at her from behind a long table. Harp stood in her green dress, her arms at her sides, her right toe extended as the music for her hornpipe began. And a banner on the side wall read 25TH ANNUAL QUAD CITIES FEIS.

*No*, thought Harp. *This isn't possible! The Quad Cities Feis is two weeks away!*

Far out among the spectators stood Mealla, smiling, nodding in encouragement. Harp felt the familiar chill that often accompanied the appearance of the Irish witch, and she realized how utterly powerless they all were against her sorcery. It had taken every ounce of Oen's power to keep a plane aloft for twenty-four hours across an ocean, yet the Kylock had undone it all, transporting her across time and space in an instant. The Irish witch's power was greater by far. There was nothing at all that Harp could do.

Except dance.

# 18

"And the winner of the Preliminary Champion competition is . . ."

Harp's eyes had closed before the female announcer had begun speaking. She already knew who the winner would be. Twelve other girls had already been summoned forward to receive their awards in her age group. But Harp's name had not been among them.

Three months ago, she would have laughed at the idea that she might qualify for Preliminary Champion so quickly—or at all. And even if she had imagined herself on a stage with other PC dancers, it would not have surprised her in the least to hear her name missing when the place-winners were recited.

But this was not three months ago.

Today Harp possessed a stunning green solo dress, had raced through the Novice and Open levels of competition in mere weeks, and had no idea how she had made the journey from Scotland to Davenport, Iowa in the blink of an eye earlier that very afternoon.

Perhaps there was a logical explanation for it all.

". . . Harp McCardle!" boomed the amplified voice.

Applause. Harp opened her eyes, smiled broadly, stepped to the center of the group of award-winners where a man in a suit handed her a trophy the size of a cello.

No. There was no logical explanation.

Harp had dreamed of this moment for years. To win a PC competition . . . why, to do that would be more than amazing. She had imagined how she would scream with joy, hold the trophy high above her head, dance a wild victory dance with her best friend, Sammy.

This was nothing like her dream. Sammy refused to speak with her. Harp's best friend felt that using the magic of the dress to win feiseanna was wrong—and dangerous. And while winning the feis was certainly thrilling, only part of the thrill seemed to come from her victory. The other part was linked to the fear of what her victory might mean.

The end of the world.

As this thought crossed Harp's mind, she caught a glimpse of Mealla in the crowd. Blonde, beautiful, smiling, and so young. And also—according to Oen, the twelve-year-old boy who had magically flown her to Scotland—an evil witch. Harp shivered and then, as the award winners began to scatter back to their camping areas, she was pulled into a hug by Miss O'Farrell, her dance teacher.

"Harp," said Miss O'Farrell, pulling back and holding the young dancer in front of her as if appraising a diamond, "you continue to amaze me! You were perfect today!"

Harp blushed uncomfortably. "Thanks, but I'm really not that good."

Miss O'Farrell hardly seemed to hear Harp's reply. "When is your next feis?"

"Two weeks," said Harp softly. "Madison."

Miss O'Farrell's eyes sparkled. "That's the second week in September. You know, if you dance as well in Madison as you did today, we'll be moving you up to the Champion level!"

Harp knew. She nodded, mustering a weak smile.

After Miss O'Farrell slipped off to offer words of encouragement to other dancers, Harp scanned the room, hoping that she had been wrong about Sammy. *How can she stay away? It's my first trophy in PC! And she's my best friend.*

But inside, Harp understood that Sammy would keep her distance as long as the Irish witch's dress stood between them. Instead, someone else suddenly loomed before Harp.

"Mealla!"

The tall, blonde woman smiled radiantly at Harp, beautiful and as youthful as spring. "I didn't startle you, did I? Why, you should feel nothing but happiness today! How wonderful it was to watch!"

This was normally where Harp would have muttered a thank-you. However, she said nothing at first. Then she forced herself to ask a question that she had been horribly afraid to ask.

"How did I get here?"

There. She had said it. Mealla would have to explain how Harp had been in Scotland one moment, and then on a dance stage in Iowa the next. And Harp could imagine only two possible answers. Either Mealla would admit that she had brought Harp back in order to complete her evil plan, or she would say nothing—which would confirm that there was, in fact, an evil plan to say nothing about. Regardless, the existence of an evil plan would be confirmed, and Harp would no longer be able to pretend that the magic of the dress was harmless.

"How did you get here?" Mealla seemed a little surprised by the question. "Why, the Mundane family brought you, just as they did the previous feis."

When Harp had stood behind the Scottish monastery, watching Oen tie a "clootie" to a tree near a magic well, the Quad Cities feis had been two weeks in the future. Not only had she crossed three thousand miles of ocean, but fourteen days in time as well. And if the Mundanes had brought her to Davenport, why did she not remember? What had she been doing for the past fourteen days?

"But I was in Scotland," protested Harp.

Mealla smiled with such complete and earnest understanding, that Harp almost wanted to hug her. "You're strong and beautiful and talented, Harp. The green dress helps to bring out those qualities that are naturally inside of you."

Harp took a deep breath. "But what does that have to do with—"

"Strong, beautiful, talented," repeated Mealla. "You can do anything you want to do! Harp, you love Irish dance, don't you?"

Harp nodded.

"And you want to be a champion?"

Harp had not intended to nod, but eventually found herself doing so.

Mealla pointed. "That dance stage was where you wanted to be, Harp! To feel the thrill of competition and the rush of excitement when they announced you as the winner! You're almost there, Harp! The best of the best!"

Despite herself, Harp felt the thrill growing inside of her. To be a champion . . . to be the one every dancer is talking about on the main stage . . .

Now Mealla pulled Harp close, gave her a hug. Harp sensed a vibrant, earthy energy. But there was something else: Up close, Mealla seemed no more than nineteen.

"You'll be on the Champs stage in October!" said Mealla, and then she pulled away, flashed another electric smile and disappeared into the swirling snows sweeping across the deserted landscape of icy ridges.

*Swirling snows?*

Harp blinked, and as her eyes popped open, she saw only the milling crowds of dancers and parents. Shivering, she decided to return to camp. And she had no idea where that might be.

Harp found that her mother had grounded her "for a month" after she failed to come home following the Milwaukee Feis. A part of her was glad that she had "missed" half of her incarceration—although she still did not understand how. The giant trophy from the Quad Cities competition took away her mother's breath. "I never realized you were improving so much!" said Mrs. McCardle. "I'm going to have to take off work and come to a feis one of these days."

Harp could not decide whether this sounded like a good idea.

As impressed as her mother was with the trophy, Harp remained grounded. "You missed your ride home, you wouldn't answer your cell phone, and then I had to drive to Milwaukee myself to pick you up! You're lucky I'm only grounding you for a month!"

*Was it really me that my mother picked up? Or was it some evil double created by Mealla? And if it was me, why can't I remember what happened the past two weeks?*

Rather than waste her energy on questions that did not seem to have a ready answer, Harp used her remaining two weeks of grounding to practice dance. She knew the green dress would help her whether she practiced or not, but a part of her wanted it to be more than the dress. How great to be a Champion dancer. But it would be one hundred times greater to *deserve* to be a Champion dancer.

Her Wednesday dance practice that week was the hardest she had ever worked. Everything below the hips seemed to scream as the workout came to a close. Harp sat beside the dance floor, chugging the last of her water bottle, when two of the older girls brushed past her.

"Nice job tonight," said one of the older girls.

Harp lowered the bottle and gasped, "Thanks!"

The older girl continued. "A few weeks ago, I wondered why Miss O'Farrell put you in *our* class instead of, you know, a group with less experience."

"Yeah," said the second older girl, whose hair was much darker. "But maybe you were just nervous or something."

"Something," repeated Harp.

"Anyway," the first older girl continued, "I just wanted to let you know that I think you've improved a lot." The other nodded in agreement.

Harp wished that she could capture those words and display them on the shelf in her bedroom. Somehow, they seemed more valuable than the giant PC trophy she had won the previous weekend.

# 19

Her grounding ended the Friday afternoon before the next feis.

"You stick close to the Mundanes this time," said Mrs. McCardle, handing back her cell phone. "I don't want to be taking anymore long trips."

*You think* you *took a long trip?* Harp thought.

After her mother left her room, Harp consulted her missed text messages. There was only one, sent earlier that day, and it surprised her: It was from Sammy.

**BRIDGE.**

She had not been there in months. Now that she and Sammy were starting middle school, they had cell phones and the Internet for talking. But for years, when they had wanted to share their dreams and secrets, they had come to the bridge. Of course, they had outgrown that. Or had they?

Harp texted a reply, found her bike in the garage and pedaled toward Claire Drive, which dead-ended at an abandoned gravel pit. She left her bike against a chain-link fence and took a trail through tall grass and down a hill into a wooded, marshy area. The trail wound around trees and then rose again into a thicker stand of oak, poplar and hickory, through which ran a creek about twice as wide as Harp was tall. A short wooden bridge, which had long ago supported a railroad spur that had served the gravel pit, crossed the creek here, and this was where Harp waited. A few minutes later she heard footsteps on the path and Sammy trotted to the bridge.

"So," said Harp.

Sammy bit her lip, breathing heavily through her nostrils, and then spat out, "You lied to me!"

"What?"

Sammy found a stick and threw it hard into the trees. Then she moved to the center of the short bridge and continued. "You told me that you were going to Scotland to get help to defeat the Kylock!"

"That's where I was going when I called," said Harp.

"Right!" said Sammy snidely. "It didn't look like you were doing much to defeat her at the Quad Cities Feis! You hugged her!"

"She hugged me!"

"And you won the PC competition! Why did you even dance?"

Harp shook her head and her gaze dropped to the ground. "I don't know. Suddenly I was just . . . there!"

Sammy stared at her darkly. "You're not dancing tomorrow, are you?"

Harp felt helpless. "Sammy, I've got to! You know what it's like to love dance!"

Sammy stared in disbelief.

"And I've been working so hard," continued Harp. "The older girls are actually starting to respect me!"

"But," implored Sammy, "she's evil."

Harp thought of Mealla's lovely smile, her youth—and how she had called Harp strong, beautiful and talented.

"You don't know that. The only one who thinks that is Oen, and he's just . . . strange!"

"I've been called worse!" said a voice, and Oen trotted up the path toward them.

"Oen!" cried Harp, taking a step toward him. "Where've you been?"

Oen stopped a few feet away, smiled, his hands in his pockets. "Ah, worried about me are you? Did you know that I slept for three days? Bringing that plane across the Atlantic wore me down! And then I had to bring it back afterwards!"

"So you just got back?" asked Harp.

"No," said Oen, "but it's easier for me to talk to you where there's magic. Like at feiseanna. Plenty of magic in Irish dance and music."

Sammy looked around. "Is there magic here?"

Oen shrugged. "More than in your school lunchroom. Why do you think you and Sammy always came here to share your secrets?"

Harp frowned. "How did you know that?"

"It's not important *how* I know," said Oen. "It's *what* I know that's significant. And I know you can't dance at that feis tomorrow."

"If I do, the world will end, right?" asked Harp haughtily.

"No," replied Oen, "but it'll take you a step closer."

"You don't understand," protested Harp. "I'm just starting to get good. And I'm almost in Champs!"

"I do understand," said Oen. "And it scares me."

"Wait a minute," said Sammy, struggling to keep up. "Does this mean Harp really was in Scotland?"

"Briefly," replied Oen. Then he turned back to Harp. "We've got to put a stop to this now. If you win tomorrow, you'll be in Champs. And if you dance in

Champs on Samhain, well, you'd better have electric socks with a ten-centuries supply of batteries."

Sammy scowled. "Samhain?"

"Halloween!" clarified Oen. "It's when the Cailleach works her evil magic on the world!"

Harp gasped. "Mealla said I'd dance in Champs in October!"

Oen nodded. "On Samhain! That's exactly what she wants!"

It seemed odd to Harp that as Oen said this, she observed a wisp of vapor escape from his mouth. Then she noticed she could see Sammy's and her own breath as well. She peered over the rail on the bridge to see a thin crust of ice beginning to form on the slow-moving creek. Overhead, the leaves and branches of the trees began to crackle as they seemed to grow their own icy coating.

"This can't be good," said Oen, glancing around nervously.

"What's happening?" cried Sammy.

Then Harp saw her, following the path through the woods just as the rest of them had come, the ice growing thicker on everything at her approach.

"Don't listen to them, Harp," said Mealla gently, ascending the rise and stopping within twenty feet of the group. "Don't you want to be the best?"

"Yes!" said Harp enthusiastically. "But I don't want to hurt anyone!"

"The seasons will change with or without you, Harp," said Mealla, smiling reasonably. "Autumn has always followed summer. And winter has always followed autumn."

"But not a one thousand-year winter!" shouted Oen.

Mealla's eyes flashed a pure hatred that twisted her features. Oen fell to his knees, his hands clutching his chest.

"Don't!" screamed Harp, and now she noticed that Sammy had doubled over, one hand pressed against her abdomen. "What are you doing?"

As Harp watched, both of her friends began to change. They seemed to grow taller, somewhat heavier, as if they had been accelerated into adulthood. Then they grew slender, hair graying, wrinkles multiplying, dark circles growing around the eyes as they receded into their skulls.

"Stop!" cried Harp. "Don't hurt them! I'll do anything!"

Oen and Sammy looked a century old, mere skeletons draped in a stubborn shroud of translucent, blotchy skin. They would crumble into dust and bone fragments in less than a minute. Yet, when Mealla's young face turned on Harp, the malice in it burned far uglier than the ravages of age upon her friends.

"You'll dance tomorrow?" cried the witch, her voice high like the screech of a great bird.

"Yes!"

"And on Samhain?"

Sammy's eyes rolled back, exposing the whites and she fell to the ground.

"Yes! Yes! Just stop!"

A swirl of mist burned away in front of Harp and, as she looked around, she saw that the trees had lost their icy sheath. She swung around to see Oen standing where he had been, rubbing his eyes as if confused. Sammy raised her head, sat up on the ground, hugged her own shoulders and shivered. Harp ran to them, embracing both simultaneously in the now eerily quiet forest.

The Irish witch seemed to have vanished with the frost.

Harp turned to Sammy. "I'm so sorry! Sorry for everything! I don't know what I would have done if anything had happened to you!"

The two girls embraced.

"I thought we were goners!" said Sammy.

"Me, too!" Harp smiled. "I'm just glad you're both okay. But I don't know what to do! I have to dance or she'll hurt you! Oen, there has to be something we can—"

The words caught in her throat as she turned to address him. Oen lay on the forest floor, as cold and silent as a stone.

# 20

"You almost died!"

Harp cupped a hand over her own mouth. It seemed a silly gesture, for there was no one to hear. She and Sammy were alone in the woods.

Almost alone.

They struggled to carry the limp form of a twelve-year-old boy. Oen was not dead, but the two girls could find no way to wake their friend, who had collapsed just moments after the Cailleach had disappeared.

"There's a big difference between almost dead and dead!" grumbled Sammy, readjusting herself under Oen's left arm. "I swear, he must weigh five hundred pounds!"

Harp labored under the other arm. Oen's feet dragged uselessly along the darkening, leaf-strewn path. She spoke in a low hiss. "Keep your voice down! The Cailleach! She might hear!" Her eyes continued to dart off into dark areas, wondering whether the vile witch who had attacked them at the old bridge was listening in—and whether she might swoop down upon them again if their chatter seemed too rebellious.

"If I were dead," continued Sammy, oblivious to Harp's pleas, "I wouldn't be able to help you!"

"You can't help me," argued Harp. "Mealla is too strong! You've got to stay as far away from me as possible! I mean, once we get done carrying Oen."

"I won't be any safer if I stay away," Sammy retorted. "If you dance, the entire world is doomed! So the safe thing is to help you find a way to avoid dancing!"

They arrived at the Claire Drive dead-end and retrieved their bikes from the brush. Being out of the woods made Harp feel a bit safer, but now she had no idea what to do with Oen. Sammy lightly patted his cheeks, begging him to wake up.

"He's breathing," she observed. "Maybe it's some kind of coma."

"We can't just leave him here," said Harp. "Can we?"

"Well, you said he has magical powers," said Sammy. "So he'd probably be okay."

"But what if the Cailleach's spell at the bridge took away his powers?" argued Harp. "You know, like Superman and Kryptonite?"

They resolved to prop him onto one of the bicycles, although he kept slipping off the seat and slouching over the handlebars like a rag doll.

"This is going to take forever!" cried Harp. As a matter of fact, it took just less than two hours to reach Harp's house—well after dark. It took another half an hour to sneak Oen into Harp's room through the window.

"I'll stay here," said Sammy, settling on the floor next to Harp's bed and pulling out her cell phone. "I'll tell my mom I'm sleeping over!"

"But I'm just getting over being grounded!" said Harp. Her mother had grounded her for a month when she had failed to come home on time after the previous feis. She had no idea what her mother would do if, on her first day of being un-grounded, she discovered that Harp had snuck a boy into her room and was having an unauthorized sleepover with Sammy.

Or if she discovered Harp had been battling witches in the forest, for that matter.

Sammy smiled. "Your mother doesn't have to know I'm here."

Harp shook her head and exited through the window in order to make her entrance at the front of the house without a magical, comatose boy. She came in through the kitchen, where her mother sat at the table. The look on her mother's face said everything.

But this did not stop her mother from translating.

"Two hours late!"

"Do you know how worried I was?"

"How could you do this—again? The very day you get un-grounded!"

"If you thought you were grounded before . . ."

The lecture seemed to go on for almost as long as it had taken to get Oen back from Claire Drive. It ended with her mother rubbing her forehead and issuing what, in Harp's world, amounted to a death sentence: "And if you think you're going to that feis tomorrow, think again! You're staying home and I'll have plenty of jobs around the house for you—all day!"

Harp trudged off to her room. But for the first time, she felt hopeful. Would the Mom Factor be enough to keep her out of tomorrow's feis? Was a mother's word more powerful than the Cailleach?

It was possible, she thought. Mothers always seemed to be coming to the rescue in storybooks. Of course, this was her real life, but at least it was something.

After she closed herself in her room, she spoke in hushed tones, sharing this theory with Sammy.

"Maybe," said Sammy, "but we need to have a backup plan. There's got to be some way to block the Cailleach's magic. You know . . . a charm or crystals or garlic."

Harp sighed. "She's not a vampire!"

"But she's got to have some weakness," argued Sammy.

"What makes you so sure?"

"Well," continued Sammy, "if she were all-powerful, she wouldn't need your help, would she?

It was true. Mealla needed help to carry out her plan. If she needed help, she was not all-powerful. Logically, there must be things that were more powerful than the Irish witch. She could be beaten.

"But how do we find out her weakness?"

Now Sammy smiled. "How does anyone find anything?" She popped off the floor and moved to the computer on Harp's desk.

"But I'm grounded!" gasped Harp. "I can't use the computer when I'm grounded!"

Sammy gave her the You-must-be-the-village-idiot look. "You've got a boy in your room, you're battling an evil witch and the fate of the world rests in your hands! You've really got to get your priorities straight!"

Her eyes traveled to the motionless boy, and she moved to sit on the mattress beside him. "Do you think he's ever going to wake up?"

Sammy's expression softened noticeably. "I don't know. For some reason, the spell seemed to take more out of him than it did me." For a moment, Sammy rested her chin on her knuckles. "You told me that Oen was looking for someone named Brighde, and that she could help."

"I don't have any idea how to find her," admitted Harp. "And I don't think Oen knows either." She glanced again at the sleeping boy.

An hour evaporated. Harp emerged from her room mostly to keep her mother from paying a visit. She apologized, which led to a repeat of portions of the previous lecture, delivered this time in a somewhat more subdued tone. Then Mrs. McCardle reheated a slice of pizza, an egg roll and a glass of milk for her daughter. When Harp arrived at the room, Sammy's eyes grew wide.

"I'm starved!"

Each consumed half a pizza slice and an egg roll half. Then Sammy motioned to the glowing screen. "Check this out. I didn't get much help when I typed Mealla—which is what the Kylock calls herself—into the search engine. But then I tried Kylock, only I spelled it the gaelic way, Cailleach."

"The Celtic goddess of winter," said Harp, reading from the web page. "Sounds like she's the most powerful goddess."

"Not quite," interrupted Sammy. She clicked onto a new page. "Brighde is the one who's supposed to defeat the Cailleach!"

Harp gasped. "That's what Oen's been saying. That's why he's been looking for her! Does it tell where to find her?"

Sammy frowned. "It says something here about wells. Hm, this is interesting."

"What?"

"Brighde has a brother named Oengus!"

Both turned toward the sleeping boy on the bed.

"What does the computer have to say about Oengus?" asked Harp.

Sammy's fingers flew across the keyboard and then she squinted at the display. "It says he's the god of love!"

Harp looked again at the boy on the bed, only this time she blushed.

"So he needs his sister to defeat the Cailleach," said Sammy, returning her gaze to the screen.

"But what if we can't find his sister in time?" asked Harp. "Is there something we can do? Some weapons we can use?"

Sammy squinted. "It says here that three things are needed to defeat the Cailleach: the sun, the dew and the rain."

Harp blinked. "That's all springtime stuff. Spring triumphs over winter."

Sammy nodded.

"But we can't wait until spring," said Harp.

"Nope," said Sammy, shaking her head.

"And if I dance, there isn't even going to be a spring!"

Now Sammy nodded again. "Yup."

"And we can't find Brighde!"

"Nope."

Harp sighed. "I never thought I'd say this, but I've never wanted to stay grounded so badly in my whole life!"

# 21

Sammy woke first the morning of the Kalamazoo Feis. The view from Harp's window showed the sun well above the horizon. Rolling over, she checked the foot of the bed where Harp had spread a blanket for herself on the floor. A wide smile spread across Sammy's face. Harp lay huddled beneath the blanket, breathing deeply.

Harp had guessed right. Her mother's word had been more powerful than Mealla's magic. The Cailleach had not been able to magically whisk Harp to the feis. Mealla could be beaten!

Sammy stood, pulling her own blanket around her shoulders. Then she settled onto the edge of the bed. Oen was still asleep. She rocked his arm, spoke softly into his ear, sighed. They would find a way to help Oen. If they could thwart magic powerful enough to transport Harp across an ocean, they would find a way to wake this boy.

Sammy had been scheduled to dance at the Kalamazoo Feis, too. She retrieved her phone. She would text her mother, tell her that she had an upset stomach, that she wasn't up to going to the feis. Then she and Harp could find a way to hide Oen from Harp's mother.

She dropped to the floor, scooted to the foot of the bed and patted Harp's blanket. Only now the blanket was flat against the floor. Harp had been there only a moment ago. Sammy would have noticed if she had opened the door to leave the room. Her eyes searched frantically, but the only other person in the room was Oen.

Harp was gone.

As the dance music concluded, Harp already knew. She could tell from the reaction of the crowd, from the way she had felt during her two steps.

She had won the PC competition at the Kalamazoo Feis.

She was now in Champs.

She felt the way a person feels in a dream, though not a pleasant dream. She could not remember waking up that morning, traveling to the feis or putting on the magical dress. Her eyes had simply opened and she had been standing beside the PC stage, feeling defeated and afraid.

Harp guessed that was how the previous owner of the dress, Kira, had felt on that day months ago when Harp and Sammy had first spied her on the PC stage. If Kira had danced that day, would Mealla have already blanketed the world in snow and ice?

But Kira had not danced. She had run from the stage. From what Harp had observed, Kira had no plan. The dress could not be destroyed. And Mealla would have found her eventually. Passing the dress along to Harp had merely delayed the inevitable.

*I could have run*, thought Harp. But she had not. Partly it was because she knew that she could not outrun Mealla. It would have been a useless, wasted effort. And she did not want to pass this horrible responsibility on to some other poor dancer.

But there was something else. Something she hardly dared admit to herself.

She liked winning.

Yes, she knew that every time she won, this increased Mealla's power. She knew that every victory brought the world closer to extinction.

But there was something intoxicating about the dress, about its ability to bring her success. She supposed it was like a man who owns a factory that makes him millions of dollars, and he keeps the assembly lines going even though he knows that fumes from its smokestacks will shorten his life and the lives of everyone who lives nearby.

*Am I really that kind of person? Or is the magic of the dress twisting my thoughts?*

The awards ceremony had been a blur, and then Mealla had been standing before her, sweet and beautiful, smiling the way a best friend might smile, looking only a few years older than Harp herself.

"Strong, beautiful, talented," said Mealla, repeating a phrase she had used before with Harp. "You can do anything you want to do! You've done it, Harp! You're in Champs! The best of the best!"

This was not how the moment was supposed to feel.

Mealla reached out, took Harp's hand. Harp's head shot back the way it might have if she had been electrocuted. The hotel ballroom where the feis had been churning along suddenly darkened, and then the walls ripped away as if torn by hurricane winds. People lay injured beneath fragments of brick, glass and steel that were quickly covered with a thin layer of snow. The buildings around her in Kalamazoo grew coatings of ice. Windows shattered in the intense cold. Snow drifts buried automobiles and busses. The Kalamazoo River froze to the bottom and erupted into jagged boulders of ice. Birds dropped from the sky onto the solid surface of Lake

Michigan. And then there was silence, as profound and awful as an evil laugh.

Mealla pulled away and the feis ballroom returned, warm and secure. Dancers laughed, packed their bags, held up awards to be photographed, munched on giant pretzels. Mealla continued to smile, and now Harp could see the cruel edge to her expression.

No, this was not how it was supposed to feel at all.

"Did I say that you were grounded for a month?" Her mother's voice rose higher, became more menacing. "Oh, it's going to be a lot longer than that! Until Christmas? Think again! Easter? Ha! You're grounded until summer vacation! In fact, there may not be any summer vacation for you, Harp!"

Harp sighed. If her mother only knew how true those last words would be.

Mrs. McCardle had discovered that Sammy had slept over even though Harp had been grounded. And that Harp had "snuck off" to go to the feis in Kalamazoo—although Mrs. McCardle had not yet determined who had given her daughter a ride. The only wee bit of good fortune was the Oen had disappeared before Mrs. McCardle had blundered into the room.

"Maybe this means he came out of his coma!" Sammy suggested when they talked at school, for both girls were forbidden to use phones or computers at home as a result of their criminal complicity.

Harp hoped Oen had recovered, although a part of her remained anxious, wondering whether magical people simply disappeared when they died.

Other than school, Harp's only activity outside of the house was Irish dance classes, which her mother allowed her to continue because they were already paid for. Harp worked harder than ever. It seemed silly to her, in a way—perhaps insane at this point—but she wanted people to think she deserved being a Champion dancer. Even if she would only dance in Champs once.

And then the world would end.

"But no Halloween Feis," her mother warned. "If I have to handcuff you to the stove, I'll do it!"

Harp knew that her mother didn't own handcuffs. Even if she did, it wouldn't matter. Mrs. McCardle could use handcuffs, chains, a concrete cell, security cameras. Mealla had an answer for everything.

*But she needs my help,* Harp kept reminding herself. *There has to be a way to defeat her.*

Her dance instructor, Miss O'Farrell, did not know that Harp had been grounded. "You must be very excited about your first feis as a Champs dancer!"

*You have no idea,* Harp thought.

As is always the case, time passed swiftly and the Halloween Feis—Samhain—drew near.

Still no Oen. And she and Sammy still had no plan to defeat the Cailleach—at least no plan that involved the potentially witch-neutralizing use of dew, sun and rain. *Oen's dead,* she thought, and the mere mental admission of this caused her to double over in sobs.

But she was wrong.

She woke very early on the morning of October 31, feeling as though she were being watched. There was Oen, standing beside her bed.

"I can't help you," he said sadly, keeping his voice low so as to not wake Harp's mother.

"Why not?" asked Harp. "You've got magic! You can do *something!*"

"I'm too weak," said Oen. "That day on the bridge, the Cailleach tried to kill your friend and me."

"No, she was just trying to get me to cooperate," Harp corrected him.

Oen shook his head. "That's how it turned out. But she was going to kill Sammy and me right there. I used my power to keep that from happening. But it drained me. I'm still not recovered."

"But what about your sister?"

"That's what I came to tell you," Oen continued. "I can't find her. You're going to have to do this on your own."

"But I don't have a sister! I don't have dew or sunshine! Or rain! I don't have a clue!"

And then the lights flickered and Harp found herself at the Halloween Feis.

# 22

Some dancers wore Halloween costumes. Harp wore the gorgeous green Irish witch's dress. She stood in line waiting to be called to the stage.

Three more dancers.

She did not want to look into the crowd, for she was afraid of what she might see. Yet, she could not resist. There stood Mealla—the Cailleach—smiling, nodding, waiting.

Hungrily.

Two dancers to go. Harp suddenly noticed that it seemed to have grown colder in the convention center. Not a lot, but somewhat. Most went on with their feis business, oblivious. And then she saw it. A thin layer of ice forming on the center's inside walls.

She wanted to bolt from the stage, but the Cailleach had too much control. There was no way she could leave. She was going to have to dance, and if she danced, she would win the competition. The green dress would guarantee that she danced better than any other dancer in the group. And when she did win, the seven golden gems would complete the witch's power, and the planet would be plunged into a 1000-year winter.

The last dancer before Harp stepped to center stage, waited for the music.

She felt useless, foolish. Sammy was right. The Cailleach must have a weakness, but they had wasted their weeks without discovering it.  Harp had never felt so worthless.

But the Cailleach had seen it differently.  "Strong, beautiful, talented.  You can do anything you want to do!"

Harp looked across the room, again saw the leering face of Mealla.  *Was she right?  Am I really that strong?*

And then she saw someone else in the crowd.  It was Sammy.  But she's grounded!  It occurred to Harp that her friend must have braved her own mother's wrath to sneak out and try to help.  Despite the awful circumstances, Harp smiled—and Sammy smiled back.  She had never been so grateful to see anyone. They had been coming to feiseanna together ever since they had begun Irish dance four years earlier.  And now, they would be together at the last feis. They had always shared a special bond.  They weren't just friends, they were almost like—

"Sisters!" Harp said the word aloud.

*You're going to have to do this on your own.*  That's what Oen had said.  He had been searching for *his* sister to help him.  But maybe Harp could get help, too.  Maybe from someone who was *like* a sister!

But what about the dew, sun and rain?  Sammy had told her those things were needed to defeat the Cailleach.

Harp looked again at her friend, whose smile gave her strength and seemed to light up the room.

*The sun!*

And as Sammy moved closer, Harp noticed tears on her friend's cheeks.

*The rain!*

Now the stage monitor directed Harp to her spot on the Champion stage.  She felt the power of the dress surging around her, but she felt another power as well: The power of her own hard work and athleticism, tensed and ready.

Harp licked away beads of sweat that had formed on her upper lip.

*The dew!*

As the music began, Harp quickly removed her right hard shoe, ripped off her poodle sock, tossed it aside and re-laced the shoe. Straightening, she tore off her competitor number and clenched it in a crumpled mass in her hand. The fiddle player gave a look as though he might stop, but Harp returned a sharp glance that clearly said, "Keep playing." And so he did.

And Harp danced.

With no chance of winning, she leapt high, pointed her toes perfectly, moved in brilliant synchronicity with the music. The green dress shimmered, more brilliantly than ever, almost too brightly to look at.

"No!" cried a voice from the crowd, a shrieking cry that transcended the music. "No!!"

Harp continued to dance, glancing when she could toward the witch, who had begun to change. The Cailleach seemed to be aging before them. The more beautifully Harp danced, the more decrepit and ancient Mealla became until, with a final screech, she exploded into a mist of ice crystals.

Instantly, the brightness on stage diminished, although the fiddle music continued. Murmurs of "What just happened?" and "Where did she go?" rumbled through the crowd. Then, their eyes began to return to the Champs stage. What they saw there was equally puzzling.

They found Harp still dancing—but wearing only shorts and a school t-shirt.

The Irish witch's dress was gone, reduced to tiny scraps and knots of thread that littered the stage.

"Why, she's just as good without the dress!" said a voice from beside Sammy, who turned to see that it was Oen.

"It's all that practice!" said Sammy, proudly. Then she gave Oen a great hug. "It's good to see you're feeling better!"

Oen smiled at her blankly. "Yes, I suppose it is. Who are you?"

"So Oen doesn't remember us at all?" asked Harp as she and Sammy sat munching nachos a short time later.

"Nope," replied Sammy. "And you'll notice his Irish accent is gone, too. But he thinks I'm cute, so we'll probably see more of him. If we ever get ungrounded."

Harp thought for a minute. "Maybe the spirit of Oenghus was working through Oen to help us stop the Cailleach." She glanced back at the stage upon which she had danced, where two elderly judges, one male and one female, were still gathering dress scraps so that dancing could resume. She knew the dress was useless now, and as far as Harp was concerned, she wanted no souvenirs of the evil thing.

Sammy's expression, meanwhile, grew pensive. "Wonder where he went? You know, the spirit of Oenghus."

Harp shrugged. "Maybe he found his sister. Just like I did!"

The two girls giggled, walked to the entrance doors of the convention center. Outside it was warm and sunny, a much nicer October 31st than usually occurs in Chicago.

# True evil can be defeated...
# ...but never destroyed.

Join Harp, Sammy and Oen as fourteen-year-olds who discover that Mealla is back. And this time, she wants more than simple world domination.

She wants revenge.

You are invited to enjoy a sneak preview from chapter one of *The Irish Witch's Tiara*, the exciting sequel to *The Irish Witch's Dress*.

Excerpt from **The Irish Witch's Tiara**

*Chapter One*
# The Impossible Rescue

Nothing in the world could have prepared Dr. David Turner for the sound that greeted him as he steered his dogsled along the edge of a jagged ice chasm fewer than one hundred miles from the North Pole.

At first, he thought it might be a trick of the wind. Then he had brought the dogs to a stop, signaling with a hand gesture for the sled behind him, manned by Dr. Peter Engstrom, to do the same. The two had started out just after dawn, placing sensing equipment at precisely calculated coordinates. Now it was just past noon. The sun glared at them without any betrayal of warmth. The air temperature registered ten degrees Fahrenheit, although the stinging wind made it feel thirty degrees colder.

That was why it made no sense. Turner could have sworn he had heard someone crying out, calling for help. To have heard such a thing above the whooshing of the sled and wind seemed almost impossible, yet he had heard it three times. Now, with the team at a stop, he listened again, pushing aside the fur-lined hood on his heavily-insulated parka and leaning into the wind. He expected to hear nothing except the shuffling of his dogs' paws and the low whistle of the gale, but then, there it was again, this time much clearer, unmistakable:

"Oh, help me! Anyone, please help!"

Turner wondered whether he might be hallucinating. Such things were not impossible in arctic extremes, although they were usually the result of hypothermia or other consequences of exposure, which he was sure he did not have. Yet, what other explanation was there? No one else could be in this remote location on the planet. Only scientists or occasional military patrols came this far north. And the voice he had just now heard had not sounded like that of a scientist.

It had sounded like the voice of a little girl.

As he listened, he heard muted crying, followed by: "I want to go home! Please!"

He turned to the man on the sled behind. "Peter, did you hear that?"

Engstrom nodded, but he needn't have. His wide eyes confirmed that he was thinking the same insane thoughts as his friend.

"How is this possible?" shouted Engstrom. "That sounds like a kid! But there's no sled! No helicopter! No ski tracks!"

Turner had already wondered these same things. They could see to the horizon in all directions. Blinding white, except for the robin's egg sky. The ice to the south was mostly smooth, but in front of them, great slabs had buckled in some spots and deep crevasses snaked between them. Their dogsleds were the only signs that humans had ever visited this desolate place. It made no sense that there should be someone else here. Adding to the mystery was the fact that, if the child had been stranded out here for any length of time, she should have been dead.

"Help! It's so cold!"

"Come on!" said Turner. The men ordered their teams down and stepped off the sleds, moving toward the crevasse.

"Hello!" shouted Engstrom.

"Where are you?" added Turner.

The men heard a hopeful squeak and then: "I'm here! I'm down in the hole!"

The men moved toward the edge cautiously, but it was difficult to see—and dangerous. They knew that a wedge near the lip could break off as they stood upon it, plunging them deep into the earth. Returning to the sleds, they retrieved stakes, pounded them deep into the ice and then secured a sled to them. Next, they tied a rope to the sled and wound it around Turner's waist. With Engstrom at the sled, letting out rope, Turner cautiously advanced. He got down on his hands and knees as he neared the crevasse and peered over the edge. What he saw made the whole episode seem even more bizarre.

About fifty feet down, a snow-blonde girl who looked to be about eight years old, stood on an ice ledge barely two feet wide. Below her, the dark maw of the crevasse disappeared into a twisting blue-black abyss. She appeared uninjured and wore no winter gear whatsoever—only a simple, white dress.

*How is she alive?* wondered Turner. He was a grown man, used to spending long periods in arctic surroundings, yet, he knew that if he removed his parka and other protective gear, he would be dead in less than half an hour.

Something was not right. Turner felt a wave of dread wash over him. What he was seeing defied the laws of nature. Yet...

"Oh, please hurry!"

*Get ahold of yourself!* He shook off his misgivings. *You've got to save her.* "What's your name, honey?"

"Ella," said the girl, beginning a soft whimper.

Turner nodded. "Ella, you just don't move. Stay close to the wall. I'm coming down to get you!" He tossed the extra rope over the edge, made a signal to Engstrom, and eased himself over the side. Although Turner was tethered to the rope, he still felt more afraid than he'd ever been. Working in sub-freezing temperatures at the top of the world carried its share of risks, but the two men usually found themselves prepared for whatever difficulties they encountered. Climbing into an ice chasm, on the other hand, was new and frightening, a challenge for which Turner felt ill-prepared—and that terrified him. What if the little girl lost her balance and fell before he reached her? What if his weight collapsed the ledge? What if the girl panicked when he tried to help her and sent them both tumbling into the darkness?

He knew this last scenario was unlikely, for he would always be tied to the rope. And the heavy sled, held in place by steel spikes, wasn't going anywhere. What he felt was simply the kind of stress that often stoked people's irrational fears.

And yet...

Who was this girl? Where had she come from? How was she still conscious, dressed as lightly as she was? And wasn't it miraculous that she had fallen fifty feet without sustaining an injury, somehow landing on a narrow ledge and not caroming off into the void. Something did not add up. And these incongruities made him even more anxious than the climb down the icy wall.

*Don't be a fool. She's just a little girl. There's an explanation. It may even be something quite simple.*

Yet, none of the many explanations swirling through his mind made any sense.

A minute later, his boots reached the ledge. He shouted this to Engstrom, and then the tiny girl embraced him tightly. For a moment, he wondered if she would ever let go. His fears vanished. The explanation, he realized, could wait. It would make sense, whatever it was. Finally, she relaxed her grip and he grabbed her shoulders, looking her directly in the eyes.

"Ella, listen carefully. Dr. Engstrom can't lift both of us, and I can't climb if I have to carry you, so I'm going to tie this rope around you. Then Dr. Engstrom will pull you up. After that, I'll climb up. Do you understand?"

Ella nodded, and then stood patiently while Dr. Turner created a loop that passed under her arms.

"Ready?"

Ella nodded again, and Turner gave a shout. The slack slowly disappeared and Ella began to rise, a few feet at a time. Finally she reached the top and disappeared over the edge. Turner waited for the rest of the slack to disappear, which would mean that Engstrom had readied the rope for him to climb out. It seemed to take a long time, which Turner chalked up to Engstrom finding something warm in which to wrap the child.

To pass the time, Turner anxiously surveyed his surroundings. The chasm appeared to be about twelve feet wide. He could not guess its depth, since the bottom was not visible. The silver-blue walls shot up at such a severe angle and with so few footholds that it would have been impossible for the child to climb out on her own. He shivered, partly due to the cold, and partly at the thought of how hopeless a situation it would be to actually find oneself stranded in such a place. However she had gotten here, she was very lucky that the two scientists had stumbled upon her.

He flinched suddenly as something dark shot past him on the left. Turner caught only a suggestion of its shape out of the corner of his eye, and by the time he looked down into the chasm, whatever it was had already disappeared into the darkness.

*Oh no! Ella!* Had she wandered back toward the edge and fallen? Turner's heart raced.

"Peter! Peter! What happened? Is the girl okay? Peter!"

He waited for a reply, telling himself to calm down. Perhaps a chunk of ice had broken off, and that's what he had seen out of the corner of his eye. Or the wind had caught a blanket from one of the sleds and blown it over the edge.

Then a small face framed by blue sky appeared overhead.

*Thank God!*

"Honey, move back away from the chasm!" called Turner, attempting to control his breathing. "Tell Dr. Engstrom to let me know when the rope is secure!"

Ella smiled. Turner noticed she still was wearing no blanket or protective gear—just the simple white dress. His mouth went suddenly dry and his stomach began to churn uneasily. Then a stab of white-hot terror pierced him as he saw her hold up the other end of the rope.

"Dr. Engstrom isn't here," said Ella good-naturedly. "And I don't know anything about knots. So here."

With that, she tossed the loose end of the rope over the edge. Turner cried out in horror and then braced himself so the weight of the rope didn't pull him off the ledge when it unwound. The weight of it jerked his torso as if someone had tossed him a bowling ball, but he had been ready for it, had leaned hard into the wall and had managed to keep his footing. When he felt steady, he looked up in disbelief, at the impish, smiling face.

"Peter!" he shouted hoarsely. There was another rope. In a moment, his colleague would lower it. But they needed to protect the little girl. "Peter! Get her away from the chasm!"

The girl giggled. "I told you. Dr. Engstrom isn't here."

"That's ridiculous. Where—"

Then he remembered the falling object and he began to shiver uncontrollably.

"Help! Help!"

He realized immediately that calling out was useless, for there was no one within miles. Yet, in his panic, he could not help himself. He attempted to slow his breathing again. "Ella! Ella, you've got to help me!"

"My name is actually Mealla. Ella is just a nickname."

"All right Mealla, I need you to go to my sled and find the other rope coil. Tie one end to my sled, really tight! Use lots of knots!"

"I'm going to be using your sled to take me away from here," said Mealla as if discussing the weather. "I'm still kind of weak. I've been trapped here for two years!"

The child had to be insane. How she had come to be here he would figure out later. Right now, he had to find some way out of the chasm.

*My radio!*

He and Engstrom each carried the devices so that they could communicate with each other, and so that they could call for help in case of emergencies. This was definitely an emergency. He reached into the pocket of his parka where he normally kept it.

It wasn't there.

The hope drained from him.

"Are you looking for this?" Mealla playfully held up the radio.

"How—" Then Turner remembered the long hug she had given him when he had arrived on the ledge.

"Want it?" she asked playfully, dangling it over the edge. "Catch!" She dropped the radio. He watched it sail past, just beyond his reach, and clatter to pieces against the dark walls of the chasm.

"Too bad!" she giggled. "Well, I'm leaving now! Thank you for rescuing me, Dr. Turner. I couldn't have gotten out by myself. They took all my powers away. Except the immortality. But whenever someone else loses, I gain. And because of you and Dr. Engstrom, I'm now feeling more powerful already! I've still got a long way to go, but I want you to know that you have been a big help. In fact, you can be certain that what you've done today will change the world!"

"I—I don't understand..."

"You don't need to understand," said Mealla, her ominous words sounding completely inconsistent with her elfish body and childish face. "Simply be grateful that you had the opportunity to look into the face of the most powerful being in the world before you died!"

With that, the face disappeared from the opening. For a few moments, Turner heard the clanking of the sled and the movement of the dogs.

Then there was only cold and the whistling of the wind.

The *Irish Witch's Dress* was originally published as a serialized novel in *Feis America Magazine* between October 2008 and October 2009.　It has been expanded for publication here as a novel.

## Acknowledgements

Thanks to My Lovely Wife Marsha, my greatest fan, friend and passion.

Thanks to my daughter, Haley Marie, whose inspiration has helped me to bring Irish dance to life in these books.

Thanks to Kathleen O'Reilly-Wild, former editor of Feis America Magazine, for the opportunity to first offer The Irish Witch's Dress in her publication. She continues to be a tireless promoter of Irish dance and a fond friend.

Thank you to everyone who helped in ways big and small. Even if you were not named here, please know that I am enormously grateful for your contributions.

## About the Author

Rod Vick has written for newspapers and magazines, has worked as an editor and has taught writing workshops and classes over the span of a quarter century. His short stories have appeared in a variety of literary magazines and have won both regional and national awards. He has written many novels about Irish dance and was also the 2000 Wisconsin Teacher of the Year.

Rod Vick lives in Mukwonago, Wisconsin with his wife, Marsha, and children Haley and Joshua. An occasional speaker at conferences and orientation events, he also runs marathons, enthusiastically supports his children's dance, music and soccer passions, and pitches a pretty mean horseshoe.

Made in the USA
Middletown, DE
24 November 2019